MURDER IN THE MANGROVES

A Mango Bay Mystery

Other books by Marty Ambrose:

The *Mango Bay Mystery* Series:

Peril in Paradise
Island Intrigue

MURDER IN THE MANGROVES

•

Marty Ambrose

AVALON BOOKS
NEW YORK

Published by Avalon Books, an imprint of
Thomas Bouregy & Co., Inc.
160 Madison Avenue, New York, NY 10016

Library of Congress Cataloging-in-Publication Data

Ambrose, Marty.
    Murder in the mangroves / Marty Ambrose.
        p.   cm.
    ISBN 978-0-8034-7798-8 (hardcover : acid-free paper)
    1. Women journalists—Fiction.   2. Murder—Investigation—
Fiction.   3. Florida—Fiction.   I. Title.
    PS3601.M368M87 2010
    813'.6—dc22
                                            2010018145

PRINTED IN THE UNITED STATES OF AMERICA
ON ACID-FREE PAPER
BY HADDON CRAFTSMEN, BLOOMSBURG, PENNSYLVANIA

Acknowledgments

As always, I would like to thank my family, especially my husband, Jim, for being supportive of my mystery-writing career. They are constantly there to offer advice, revisions, and good cheer!

My gratitude also extends to my friends and, in particular, Joan Van Glabek, for her upbeat attitude and keen proofreading talent.

And, lastly, I'm eternally thankful for my agent, Roberta Brown. I love having you in my corner!

Now, the mango in its infinite variety
possesses charms as engaging as
those of Cleopatra.

E. J. Banfield, *My Tropic Isle*

Chapter One

W ho would've thought when I, Mallie Monroe, awakened to the bright Florida sunshine that by the end of the day I'd wind up knee-deep in swamp water and death?

My life at the Twin Palms RV Resort on Coral Island had settled into the quiet comfort of midsummer. No hordes of tourists, no cold spells, and, most of all, no boring elementary-school stories to write for the newspaper. School was out. Tropical heaven. Except that it was hot, hot, hot.

I'd even received a raise from the *Coral Island Observer*, where I work as a reporter. Not that it amounted to much, but I actually could afford to buy new summer clothes instead of the usual "pre-owned" items I picked up at the secondhand store. Ah, the smell of fresh cotton . . . nirvana.

Yes, life was good.

And it promised to be even better. I'd received an e-mail that morning from my long-lost but not forgotten hunky ex-boyfriend, Cole Whitney. A freelance photographer, he had the kind of surfer-dude looks and free-spirited spontaneity that

I'd found irresistible at the time. We'd spent a year together in Orlando. Fun, carefree, happy times.

Unfortunately, his free spirit had urged him out west to "find himself," leaving me in a state of indentured servitude at the Magic Kingdom. I hadn't heard from him since—except for the occasional postcard. Almost two years, three months, and four days ago. But who's counting? I should've been furious with him, but being angry with Cole was like chasing a butterfly in the wind. Pointless.

Besides, I was curious to see who or what he'd morphed into on his personal-development quest. And even more curious to know if the "new" Cole still made my heart beat faster than a chorus-line tap dancer. And even *more* curious still to know how he would stack up against my attraction to island cop Nick Billie.

Perhaps a summer love triangle in the offing?

Hah.

I practically skipped into the *Observer* office that morning. It didn't take long for my bubble to burst.

As soon as I saw our secretary-cum-receptionist, Sandy, up to her elbows in a quart of double-chocolate ice cream, I knew there was trouble. She'd been on the Ozone Diet for over a year and had reached her target weight months ago, publicly stating that "hell would freeze over" before she ever gained weight again. She'd even treated herself to a makeover to go with her new slim shape: a chin-length bob for her brown hair, greenish-tinted contact lenses, and a spiffy new wardrobe.

Now, she occasionally strayed and flirted with a simple scoop of fruit-on-the-bottom yogurt, but this megadip into her favorite, forbidden dessert was full-fledged diet adultery.

"What's up?" I asked in a tentative voice.

Sandy shook her head, unable to speak. With a chocolate-laden spoon, she pointed at our editor, Anita Sanders', office.

"Oh, no. What's she done now?" I moved toward my desk. It was a rickety metal structure that barely supported the old PC I shared with Sandy. As I thumped my large canvas bag on top, the spindly legs shook with an ominous creak. By some miracle, the desk remained standing.

Sandy's shoulders drooped, and her face almost disappeared into the ice cream box.

"Drat her anyway," I muttered. Anita wasn't known for her people skills. In fact, she could be a downright nagging crone. Crusty, single-minded, and sarcastic, she'd cut her journalistic teeth at the *Detroit Free Press,* a fact she never tired of telling us. Unfortunately, she thought our little island weekly should aspire to those heights—when our biggest story last month was the purchase of a new flag for the VFW hall. I know, because I covered it. Fast-breaking news it wasn't, but, hey, that's Coral Island. Tucked in a corner of southwest Florida, the twenty-mile-long, two-mile-wide island was rural, sparsely populated, and quiet most of time—much to Anita's dismay.

"It's not Anita," Sandy mumbled between spoonfuls.

"Jimmy?" Sandy's fiancé.

Closing her eyes, she whimpered, "No."

"What, then?"

At that moment, the door to Anita's cubicle opened, and she strode out.

I blinked a couple of times in shock. "Ohmygod." My hand went to my mouth. *Not Anita. Worse.*

It was Anita's twin sister, Bernice.

Even though their faces looked exactly alike—thin-lipped mouth and aging, sun-damaged skin—I could tell them apart because Bernice weighed about twenty pounds more than Anita and sported close-cropped, salt-and-pepper (more salt, less pepper) hair. She also favored a fashion style of dress that could only be described as "tacky nautical": red tank top with a little anchor embroidered on the chest, boat-patterned Capris, and gold-plated jewelry everywhere. A geriatric sailor girl.

To call Bernice the "evil twin" would be a misnomer. An "evil" twin would suggest that the other was "good." Needless to say, Anita hardly fit into the latter category. They were both sixtyish and cantankerous, as far as I could tell. Having Anita on the island had been bad enough, but when Bernice showed up six months ago to start up a charter fishing business, people got out their garlic and crosses for protection.

"Nice to see you, too, Miss Priss," Bernice said, slipping a lollipop into her mouth, the stick protruding from between her lips like a large toothpick. Again, another notch down: Anita chewed gum like crazy, but only because she'd kicked the cigarette habit.

"My name is Mallie, as you well know." I straightened to my full five feet five and one half inches and puffed out my flat chest for all it was worth. "What are you doing here, and where's Anita?"

Bernice smiled with a feline sort of smugness. *A Cheshire crone.* "My idiot sister left to take a vacation. Do you believe that? She's never had one in the seven years she's been at the *Observer.*"

Sandy and I both nodded.

"That moron who owns the paper, Bentley—"

"Mr. Benton," I corrected, keeping an eye on the bobbing stick in her mouth.

"Whatever." She rolled her eyes. "He said by law she had to take a vacation, so she took off—and put me in charge of the paper."

"What!" For a few moments, the room began to spin. Was I dreaming? Had I entered bizarro world? "But she hates you."

"Yeah, I know. And I hate her too. But there's no one else

on this crap island she trusts to be hard-nosed enough to run things."

I sat down—or, rather, my legs gave out.

"Don't worry, Miss Priss, I won't work you too hard." She guffawed—low-pitched and throaty. *Oh, my.*

Sandy handed me a heaped spoonful of ice cream. I downed it in one gulp.

"Let's get down to business. . . . I've got some ideas to spark up this hopeless rag." Bernice strolled toward us. "Right now, the stories are as downright dull as dirty dishwater. We need some *real* juice. . . ."

I almost gagged at the simile but somehow managed to swallow the ice cream. "What did you have in mind, Bernice?"

"No school stories about bratty little kids doing stomach-turning 'good works' for the community. Spare me. Or boring Town Hall meetings where a bunch of old codgers discuss how to 'beautify the island.' Just thinking about it makes me want to stick my head into the nearest toilet and barf." She grabbed my spoon, rammed it into the ice cream box, and scooped out a small chunk. "Nope, we're going to do some real-life kind of stuff. The journalistic version of reality TV." She shifted the lollipop to one side of her mouth and downed the ice cream on the other side.

"Huh?" I didn't know what alarmed me out more—her eating the ice cream with my spoon or the implication of "reality journalism."

She smiled down at me. "You're not only going to *report* the stories, Miss Priss. You're going to live 'em. Get your hands dirty. Get your feet dirty. Dang it, you're just gonna get down and dirty." She licked the spoon. Needless to say, I wouldn't want it back again.

Sandy and I abandoned the ice cream. It now had "Bernice

cooties." Then I began to do a slow burn about the "down and dirty" suggestion.

"Bernice, I've been involved in two murder investigations and almost got myself killed both times. If that isn't getting "down and dirty," I don't know what is. I was almost shot one time and nearly stabbed the other. Not to mention having a crazed murderess try to pull my hair out by the roots." I rubbed my head for effect and galvanized my motormouth into high gear. "Let me tell you, my scalp was sore for almost a week. But I didn't complain. I just came to work and wrote the story. I do what I have to for the paper. Anita has taught me that. But she wouldn't like it if I started doing sensationalized stories that—"

"Anita ain't here. I am. And do me a favor: can the long-winded sob stories. It's not like I care." She picked up the ice cream carton and scraped out the last vestiges with my ex-spoon. "I want to make sure the word gets out to our advertisers that things are changing. We might get in some new accounts from people who've got a few bucks to spare. Like Danny's Bait Shack or the Frozen Flamingo. We need to beat the bushes and bring in some decent dollars. You know what I mean?"

Sandy and I both stared mutely at her.

"You can't simply beg them on the phone, Sandy. You need to get up-front and in their face—bully 'em." She tossed the empty box into the trash can—my ex-spoon followed. "Do whatever it takes."

"Anita always felt that people on the island wouldn't respond to a hard sell," Sandy began in a quiet voice. "That's not the way things work here—"

"Really? I say, slap 'em in the face and grab their wallets. *That* sells advertising. I should know. I kept my charter biz going in Fort Lauderdale with flyers, cheap advertising, and promotions with the girls from Scooters. I did it because it works."

Sandy's mouth clamped into a mutinous line.

"Get on the phone, sweetie. Let's make things happen." Bernice snapped her fingers several times in rapid succession. "Now!"

Sandy picked up the phone, glaring at Bernice with eyes that could shatter glass.

"Good. Now here's *your* assignment, Miss Priss." She handed me a press release. "A new hiking trail opens on Little Coral Island today. You need to get your butt out there. And I'm not talking only interviews. I want you to hike the trail with the guide, wade through the swampy waters, give a firsthand account of meeting up face-to-face with an alligator. Action. Excitement. Adventure. Let's do it. Chop-chop."

I'll give her a chop, all right, I thought to myself. *A karate chop.* I had my yellow tip in Tae Kwon Do now and could give her a hard jab right in the neck. I fantasized about doing it for a few mad moments—nothing lethal, of course. Only enough to disable her until Anita returned.

"The trail tour starts in thirty minutes." Bernice tapped her watch. "Time's a-wasting."

She strolled back into Anita's cubicle, which passed for an office, gold bracelets jangling.

Once she closed the door, Sandy buried her head in her hands and moaned.

"Hang in there. We'll find a way out of this. What we need is a plan." I sat there for a few moments, fingers drumming on my desk. *Come on, girl. You solved two murders.* "Okay, here's what we'll do. Get on the phone with Mr. Benton and see if this 'takeover' is legal. I don't see how Anita can ask Bernice to take over the paper when she doesn't have any journalistic experience."

Sandy raised her head. "You think?"

"Dunno. But Benton is a reasonable guy—maybe he'll take

pity on us. Then we'll try to find out where Anita went on her vacation, so we can tell her what Bernice plans to do. If Anita learns that her sister is damaging the newspaper's reputation, she'll get back here before you can say *key lime pie.*"

"Oh . . . tasty." Her eyes brightened.

"That was metaphorical," I cautioned. "I'm a lit major. And we have 'miles to go before we sleep,' to quote Frost." *If we're lucky.* Then again, we might not get *any* sleep while Bernice lurked around the newspaper.

"My head is spinning." Sandy raked a hand through her nut-brown hair. "Or maybe it's my stomach churning. I had three doughnuts this morning before I started on the chocolate ice cream, and I've got a bag of M&M's in my car." She pinched her upper legs, shaking her head in disgust. "I might as well just apply them directly to my thighs."

I took Sandy by the shoulders. "You're *not* going off the Ozone Diet. It took you too long to whittle down to this weight. Remember you and Jimmy are getting married in the spring. You've got to fit into that wedding dress. Be strong, sister, and ditch the candy."

"Okay." She tried to paste a slight smile onto her face. "We're in trouble, aren't we?"

"Yeah, deep trouble. But first things first—I've gotta cover the story." I grabbed my Official Reporter's Notepad, shoved it into my large canvas bag, and set out for the trail.

So much for the tropical heaven.

My battered old truck, Rusty, decided for once not to act up. I made it to the trail on Little Coral Island in less than fifteen minutes—in time for the hike and introductions. *Oh, boy.*

Little Coral Island lay situated along the inner coast of the bigger island, three miles long, with nothing but wetlands and wildlife. Scrubland. Palmetto palms. Critters. And little else.

As I climbed out of my truck, I felt the late-June heat and humidity envelop me with its morning greeting. It wasn't the kind of full-fledged embrace that squeezed the life out of you at midday. But that was coming. And with my freckled skin and supercurly red hair, I was the last one who needed to be given that kind of loving attention.

As I approached a small group near the entrance to the trail, I noticed that everyone wore hiking shorts and the ever-present Coral Island "Reeboks"—knee-length white fishing boots. I looked down at my cheapie Keds. *Uh-oh.* Not much protection there.

"Hi, glad you could join us." A young woman with shoulder-length auburn hair and thick, round glasses motioned me over. She wore a sleeveless cotton top, hiking pants, baseball cap, clip-on sunglasses, and the white boots. Obviously ready for action.

"I'm Mallie Monroe from the *Observer.*" I held up my note-pad. "I'm here to take notes and talk to you as we go down the trail."

A broad grin of uneven teeth answered me, as the woman pumped my hand in a vigorous shake. "Angela Stillwell—chief guide for the Coral Island Parks and Recreation Service. So happy to meet ya," she drawled. "Your editor, Bernice, called me this morning to let me know you'd be coming along today. You're gonna *love* it." She gave my hand one more pump.

"Thanks." I flexed my fingers.

"Well . . . to begin with, Little Coral Island is part of what we call in the South a 'preserve.'" She stressed the first syllable. "It has near to five thousand acres of unique wetlands that have been restored to their natural, native glory." Angela gestured with a wide arc of her arm across the expanse of tropical vegetation with an air of dramatic emphasis. "We've created this trail so islanders and tourists could hike, rest a spell, and just take in nature."

I jotted down these comments, amazed that anyone could get so excited about some scrubby-looking flora and fauna.

Angela turned back to the small gathering of hikers. "Would y'all like to introduce yourselves to Mallie?"

"Hi, I'm Mae Hamilton, and this cute thing is my husband, George," a gray-haired woman drawled as she pointed at the tall, wizened guy next to her. "We're here for bird sightings."

Dressed similarly to Angela, the birder duo had further accessorized themselves with sun-protective hats that looked like something out of the French foreign legion, hiking shorts, and binoculars dangling from thin leather straps around their necks.

"And I'm Charley." He waved a wrinkled, age-spotted hand and then held up a cane. "It's a hiking stick—I don't really need any help to walk." *Uh-huh.* He, too, wore binoculars.

"Are you also a birder?" I inquired.

"Yup." He thumped his chest in pride. Unfortunately, he must've used too much force, because the blow caused a coughing fit that almost doubled him over. Angela slapped him on the back a couple of times, and he straightened again.

"Now that we're near to kin to one another, let's kick up some sand and get moving." Our intrepid Dixie Chick trail guide handed each of us a small green brochure. "As you can read, the trail is almost three miles—"

"What?" Now it was my turn almost to double over, but in shock. Sure, I've been doing Tae Kwon Do a couple of nights a week, but a three-mile walk in Keds? *No way.* That was close to inhumane treatment. And in late June, with the heat and insects? Downright torture.

"You'll be fine. Just give yourself a good dousing with bug spray." Angela dismissed my concerns and pointed at her brochure. "Listen up, everyone! As we're hiking, follow along with the pictures and the explanations. They explain some of the wonderful sights we'll be seeing."

My three elderly companions all nodded in happy anticipation.

"I didn't bring any insect repellent," I protested.

"Here you go, my dear." Charley passed me his can of Bug Off!, and I layered it onto my arms and legs. The pungent smell of pine and tar assailed my senses.

"Whew. This stuff is strong," I mumbled, trying to hold my breath. I looked down at my attire in cautious hesitation. Since I'd had no idea I'd be on a sweltering, bug-infested trail walk when I dressed that morning, I had worn my standard uniform of denim shorts and T-shirt. My pale, freckled legs would be exposed to sun and bugs. I cursed Bernice under my breath.

"Mosquitoes come up like a bad cloud this time of year on the island," Angela added in a chipper voice. "But they have to live like every other creature, and I reckon we should respect them."

"As long as they're not sucking every drop of blood out of us," I quipped. Charley blinked. Mae and George shook their heads. Angela snorted. I sighed and accepted my fate.

As added protection, I gave myself one last douse of spray.

"I think you might need this too." Mae passed me a bottle of SPF 15 sunblock. It wasn't high enough, but I slathered it all over my freckled face anyway in the vain hope of not getting sunstroke. I knew I probably looked like a kid pretending to be a ghost at Halloween, but I wasn't taking any chances. My skin fried under a forty-watt lightbulb.

"Once again, let me welcome y'all to Little Coral Island," Angela began. "This is a coastal wetlands area with a salt marsh and mangroves—"

Just then a large black Mercedes drove up, and two young women alighted, talking and giggling.

"Thanks, Dad." A leggy blond leaned into the driver's side window and placed a peck on the man's cheek.

He gave her a brief smile and an arm pat. "Have fun, girls," he said. "Don't forget to call on your cell phone so I know when to pick you up."

"Will do." The blond tucked her hair behind her ears and sauntered over with her friend. Daddy drove off, tires grinding on the shell road.

"Are we too late for the tour?" her friend asked. She was striking, too, but in a different way. Raven-wing hair, brown eyes, and honey-colored skin. And lots of curves. Both girls wore T-shirts, cotton Capris, and high-heeled leather boots. Island hotties, for sure.

"Nope." Angela motioned them forward. "We were just fixin' to start out." She insisted that we introduce ourselves again, and I found out the blond's name—Brandi, with an *i,* not *y.*

"Don't you know who this is?" Brandi the Blond gestured in the direction of her friend.

"No, should we?" Mae adjusted her bifocals.

"This is Gina Fernandez—Coral Island's own Mango Queen this year." She made the pronouncement as though she were introducing the queen of England. I looked around, half expecting to hear a trumpet fanfare. But I heard only a squawking bird overhead.

Gina treated everyone to one of those model-perfect, beaming-headlight smiles, with teeth so white, it hurt to look at them. "Hiking the Little Coral Island trail is one of my first official duties as Mango Queen. It's a pleasure to be here."

A queen of mangos?

Our little group was suitably impressed, especially me. I'd never met a Mango Queen before, and an interview with Gina might give my trail story a more interesting slant. "Could I get some quotes from you after the hike? I work for the *Observer.*"

"Sure, I'd be happy to." Gina donned a wide-brimmed straw hat with a printed peachy scarf around the brim. "Everyone on the island will want to know what the Mango Queen is doing."

"Oh, yes," Brandi gushed.

"And, of course, the comings and goings of the Mango Queen runner-up." Gina slipped an arm around Brandi's shoulders. Her friend submitted to the hug, but for a moment I thought I saw a glint of envy in Brandi's eyes.

"Is this some kind of island pageant?" I asked.

"Whaaaat?" The girls both turned toward me, arms akimbo. "You don't know?" they asked in unison.

"Guess not." I spread my hands in helpless appeal.

Gina clucked her tongue. "Every year Coral Island has a Mango Festival, and an island girl is elected queen to preside over the festival and any island events." She raised her delicate chin. "It's a great honor."

"You betcha," Charley chimed in.

I could see an angle for my trail story taking shape. "Could I ask you—"

"Time for interviews later." Angela clapped her hands to get everyone's attention.

"All right," I grumbled.

We all trooped, single file, behind Angela as she led us through a narrow opening in the six-foot-high chain-link fence located at the entrance to the trail. Mosquitoes swarmed around my ankles, but the bug spray seemed to be doing its job—for now. I prayed the sunblock would keep my face from turning into a broiled lobster.

Angela motioned to the right and then left, talking all the while. "Little Coral Island is the home for many types of wildlife—birds, rabbits, wild hogs, snakes—"

"Will we be seeing any of those creatures today?" I cut in,

panicked. I don't like snakes or, for that matter, hogs or birds. I could barely tolerate rabbits. Nature Girl I was not.

"Only the birds," Angela said. "The other animals skitter out at night. But we'll be able to look at their scat."

"Their what?" Gina asked.

"Dung." Angela pointed at a dried brown lump off to one side of the trail.

Oh, goody. I was going to spend my morning looking at animal dung. I'd reached a new high in journalism. Maybe I should take pictures and have them blown up, poster-size, for Bernice.

Gina and Brandi giggled. They pulled out their cell phones and took a few pictures.

Angela leveled a severe glance in their direction. "Y'all notice we're finishing up the wetlands restoration 'round here. In the past, digging these ol' drainage ditches controlled the mosquitoes, but, unfortunately, it also caused the spread of melaleuca and Australian pines—"

Mae's hand shot up like a torpedo. "What's wrong with those trees?"

"They kill off the native vegetation."

"Oh, dear." Mae shuddered.

"Unlike this beautiful tree . . ." Angela patted a large trunk shaded by a canopy of leafy branches. It stood guard at the beginning of the trail. "That's Old Blacky—he's a grand black mangrove. Been there almost a hundred years, from what we can tell. He shelters palm warblers and other songbirds in the winter."

Everyone appeared suitably awed. I personally thought Old Blacky looked a bit like Old Decrepity but kept the thought to myself.

"Let's hit it." Angela marched off down the trail, and,

gamely, we followed. Charley clutched his can of Bug Off!;
Mae and her husband, George, clutched their binoculars; Brandi
and Gina clutched their cell phones; and I clutched my notepad.

Within the next ten minutes, though, I knew I was in trouble.
As we moved deeper into the wetlands, the ground became
increasingly mushy. My Keds sank with each step, the mud
almost to my ankles, as the sun beat down with unremitting
heat. I cursed Bernice once more under my breath.

After half an hour, we finally stopped near an outgrowth of
long grass. Everyone was panting but Angela (of course) and
Charley (amazing), who had taken the lead of our motley crew
with his "hiking stick."

"That's needlerush." Angela pointed at a plant with long,
stiff leaves.

I reached down to touch it. "Ouch." Instantly, I jerked back
my hand.

Angela treated me to the severe glance this time. "Don't
touch *anything* on the trail unless I instruct you to. Needlerush
is as sharp as a knife."

"Now you tell me." I grabbed a Kleenex out of my canvas
bag and wiped the blood off my hand. That damn needlerush
had sliced a thin cut along my palm—and it hurt like all get-
out. I gritted my teeth. Not a good sign. This was going to be
the hike from hell.

As we soldiered on, I wasn't disappointed in my prophetic
abilities. Angela stopped at every bush and plant for an ex-
haustive diatribe, including the names in both Latin and Eng-
lish. She even produced books out of her backpack to read us
further Very Important Data to raise our awareness, adding
her own genteel environmental southernisms.

Another thirty minutes or so later, I was ready to take a
bulldozer to the entire trail. I was sweaty, tired, and set to pack

it in. My feet had turned into salty, soggy lumps, my hand appeared inflamed from the close encounter with needlerush, and my skin felt as if it were sizzling in a frying pan.

Oddly, my companions seemed unfazed as they occupied themselves with other interests. The birders attempted to spot eagles, ospreys, or anything that had two wings and a beak. And the beauty queens produced a travel cosmetic kit and spent most of the hike debating the merits of powder eye shadow over cream eye shadow.

I would've zoned out myself, contemplating my upcoming reunion with Cole, if I hadn't had to take notes for my story.

At the halfway point, we edged around a buttonwood pond and took a break to bird-watch. I almost broke into a round of hallelujahs. Since I couldn't tell an ibis from a turkey vulture and, what's more, didn't care, I found myself huddling under the shade of a cabbage palm with Brandi the Blond and Gina the Mango Queen.

To my dismay, they switched subjects to exfoliators and skin serums, neither of which I used. For a few mad moments, I contemplated rejoining the birders.

But then Gina pulled out some trail mix and a plastic bag filled with fruit, and my interest perked up. I'd missed my Krispy Kreme run that morning and was starving, although I would've preferred my typical sugar-filled fare to this so-called healthy stuff. Still, hiking-trail beggars couldn't be choosers.

Gina shared a handful of the trail mix and offered me some of the fruit.

"Oranges?" I reached into the Baggie.

"Mangos—sliced fresh this morning from the grove."

Instantly, I pulled back. Being a fast-food, frozen food, or canned food kind of girl, I didn't care for anything just off the tree—and mangos were last on my list of preferred fruit, right below the watermelon. Too watery and bland.

"Try it. I promise you'll like it," Gina prompted.

Doubtfully, I helped myself to the smallest slice of the peachy-colored, slimy-looking fruit.

"You can't live on Coral Island and not eat mangos," Brandi said as she downed a large piece. "It's like . . . against the law or something."

"It should be." Gina savored a piece as if it were the finest delicacy. "You know, the mango originated in India. Its cultivation goes back four thousand years. The tree is practically worshipped there, and—"

"Like we care," Brandi teased, but I noted an edge to her voice. "You've already made Mango Queen, girlfriend. No need to keep on campaigning."

"I'm not." Gina pursed her mouth. "I happen to think it's a cool fact that Mallie might want to use in her news story."

"Sure. I just might." I flashed a phony smile as I took a tiny bite of the mango. The rest would be tossed into the pond the moment Gina turned her back.

But mid-chew, I was amazed to find my taste buds melting under the delicious onslaught of flavors—hardly bland. Clove. Cinnamon. Coconut. Fig. *Wow.* Manna from heaven. "This is incredible." I had eaten a mango only once, and it had tasted nothing like this one.

"Told ya." Gina passed me the Baggie. "Here. You can have the rest."

"Thanks." I grabbed the largest slice and gobbled it down in one swallow. "I've never tasted anything as sweet outside of doughnuts."

"It's a variety developed on Coral Island," Gina said with a touch of pride in her voice.

"Come on, ladies. This is a hike, not a picnic." Angela fluttered past us with the birders, and we fell into formation once again.

I placed the mango slices in my canvas bag and heaved it

onto my shoulder. The respite was over—back to the sun, bugs, and scat. Oh, well, at least I'd had enough of a sugar rush from the mango to jump-start my flagging energy.

Eventually, the interminable hike ended back where we'd started. I checked my Mickey Mouse watch—courtesy of my short, undistinguished tenure at Disney World. Amazingly, only a couple of hours had passed. It had seemed like ten.

While we stood near the parking lot, panting in the heat and thanking Angela, everyone produced water bottles. My mouth dropped open, too parched even to drool. Of course I had no water, and I needed it—desperately. My mouth felt as dry as the cotton balls in Marlon Brando's mouth when he played the Godfather.

"Here, honey, take mine." Mae handed me her bottle. "I'll share with George."

I couldn't speak. My gratitude was beyond words. I guzzled down almost the whole bottle in a matter of seconds.

"You'd better wash off your feet first chance you get," Mae observed, eyeing my crusty Keds. "The salt water in the marsh can strip your skin bare."

"Thanks for the tip." Mae had turned out to be my fairy godmother of trail survival.

"I've gotta run," Angela called out as she waved good-bye and climbed into her Jeep Cherokee. "Y'all feel free to come back for another hike anytime you want," she added, her head tilted out the open driver's side window.

I watched as she drove off, evaluating her vehicle. Some people like to psychoanalyze people. I liked to dissect cars. They told me a lot more about a person than the Myers-Briggs test. Dented, filled to the brim with hiking gear and environmental books—I didn't need to push my analysis of Angela's Jeep any deeper. It confirmed what I already suspected: Angela needed an intervention. She was addicted to the outdoors.

After my elderly companions and I bid one another farewell, they drove away, leaving me with the beauty queens.

"I told you that I decided to wait for Brett," Gina was saying.

"But Dad said *he'd* pick us up when we finished the hike." Brandi whipped out her cell phone.

"Pleeeeease. I'd prefer to wait for my fiancé."

"It's stupid to stand in the heat like this arguing. I'll call Dad."

"No." Gina stamped her foot. She produced her own cell phone and pressed a few buttons in rapid succession. "I just sent Brett a text message—he'll be along soon." A triumphant smile spread across her lovely face.

Brandi flipped open *her* cell phone and hit the speed-dial button. "Shoot—all I got was Dad's voice mail." She snapped the cell shut, glaring at Gina. "I'm going to walk up to the main road and try again."

"I'm staying right here." Gina folded her arms across her chest.

"Fine." Brandi spun on her heel and strode away.

Gina gave an exclamation of disgust.

We stood there in silence for a few minutes, the dueling island girls' dispute lingering like a dark cloud.

"You want me to drop you somewhere?" I finally spoke up. "Maybe I could interview you along the way."

"If you don't mind, I'll wait here. I'm out of water and kinda tired." Gina removed her straw hat and wiped a hand across her forehead. "Brett never keeps me waiting long."

I didn't doubt her. "How 'bout I get us some water and check back for a quick interview? If your fiancé picks you up in the meantime, I'll call you later with some questions."

"Great." She gave me her cell phone number. "I'll wait in the shade."

I jumped into Rusty and revved off, windows open, trying

for a bit of a breeze. My air conditioner puffed out meager breaths of cool air at best.

I rolled past Brandi. "You want a ride?"

She averted her head and motioned me on. I shrugged and turned onto Coral Island Road. I drove straight to the Circle K and bought four twelve-ounce bottles of water—two for me and two for Gina. Downing one at the checkout counter, I let the cool air in the store drain some of the heat from my body.

The newly hired, potbellied cashier, Benny, who always smelled of cheap, woodsy aftershave, handed me my receipt. "Sweetheart, your nose is the color of a beet."

I touched it. It felt warm. "Oh, no."

As I climbed back into Rusty, I checked my face in the rearview mirror. My eyes widened in horror. My skin was almost the same color as my hair. I drove to the drugstore, and, after a brief discussion with the pharmacist, I bought a small jar of healing aloe lotion. I slathered it on, using a mirror in the cosmetics department.

After purchasing the lotion, along with an extra bottle of water, I checked my watch. Close to forty-five minutes had passed, but maybe Brett the Fiancé had been held up.

I headed back toward Little Coral Island, figuring Gina might still be there. En route, I become acutely aware of a growing discomfort in my feet. My Keds finally seemed to be drying out, but they also felt as if they were hardening in the process. I glanced down and grimaced. The salt water had transformed the canvas shoes into two solid, sandy blocks. I tried to curl my toes. Not even the pinky had enough room to flex.

Gripping the wheel with one hand, I reached down with the other and tried to slip off my left shoe. It didn't budge. I'd need the Jaws of Life to get the darn things off my feet. *Great. Just great.*

A few minutes later, I turned into the empty parking lot near the Little Coral Island trail. Scanning the area for Gina, I spied her sitting under the black mangrove tree. Grabbing the water and my notepad, I set out to do the quick interview.

"Gina!" I waved at her.

She didn't respond.

"I'll trade you a water for a couple of quotes," I joked, holding up the plastic bottles.

Still no answer.

Quickening my pace, I rounded the chain-link fence. "Are you okay? This heat is killing me—" I broke off as I noticed the total stillness of her body. Her arms lay limp at her sides, her head tilted back, her eyes set in a glassy stare. A syringe nestled in the grass next to her hand.

My breath caught in my throat as I dropped the water bottles.

Gina the Mango Queen was dead.

Chapter Two

I peered at Gina, too stunned to move. She couldn't be dead.
For goodness' sake, I'd just seen her laughing and talking with
her friend. She was too young. Too full of life. Too beautiful.

My heart began to thump erratically. I reached for my cell
phone, a crazy mixture of hope and fear rising up inside of
me. Maybe she wasn't really dead. Maybe she was only rest-
ing. I checked her pulse. Oh, yeah, she was dead all right.

I punched in 911 and told the dispatcher where I was and
what had happened. After that, my legs gave out, and I sank
down to the ground next to Gina, my eyes closed to the horri-
ble reality of her death.

That's where they found us.

The ambulance, fire truck, and Detective Nick Billie all arrived simultaneously.

As Nick helped me to my feet, I watched the paramedics
check Gina's vitals. After several long minutes, they shook
their heads.

She was gone.

"Mallie, are you okay?" Nick's familiar deep voice wafted

over me like a velvet balm as he touched my arm in reassurance. Because he was Coral Island's chief deputy, I knew he'd be the one to answer the call. He'd be the one to take charge of the situation and make everything okay. But he couldn't. He couldn't bring Gina back to life.

"No, but I'll survive." My voice sounded as shaky as my legs still felt. "You know, I was doing a story—a simple story on the new Little Coral Island trail. That's all. Granted, it was hot as Hades, and my feet got soaked from all the salt water, but other than that everything seemed normal. As normal as it can when having to trudge three miles to look at animal dung and a few pathetic birds and—"

"Okay, I know you're still in shock, but try to calm down." He fastened his eyes on me—deep, dark pools of concern. "I need to know exactly what happened and how you found the body. Keep it simple and straightforward." He kept his own tone quiet and steady.

Still, a dead body sprawled on the grass only a few feet away. Could I help it that when I got nervous, I couldn't stop talking? Some people smoked. Some people drank. I talked and talked and talked.

"Okay, I'll try." I took in a deep breath and began with that morning, when Bernice had assigned me the story. I spent almost ten minutes divulging the shock of having Anita's nutty twin appear at the *Observer.*

"Could you get to the actual trail hike?" he inquired.

"All right." I started to fill him in on all the details as briefly as possible, but I was finding it hard to focus on the sequence of events. Gina's motionless body kept distracting me. I tried not to look at her, but out of the corner of my eye I could see her long brown hair flowing out from her lovely face. I stumbled over my words several times yet somehow managed to finish up.

Nick Billie took notes but said nothing until I'd finished.

Another deputy snapped pictures of the scene, and then the paramedics took Gina away. I sighed inwardly. Her image would be with me for a long time.

"Is that all you remember?" he pressed me.

"I think so. . . . Can we get out of the sun?" I brushed perspiration from my forehead. We moved under the shade of the huge black mangrove, but it still felt like an inferno. "Did you know Gina?" I asked him.

"Not really." He shrugged. "I'd heard she was elected the Mango Queen a few days ago, that's all."

"Is that really such a big deal?"

"It's Coral Island's version of the Miss America pageant. Women campaign for a solid year to win the title."

"That's odd. Anita didn't have me cover the story last year or this year." I felt my lips pucker in confusion. "She's usually so dogged about every little thing that happens on the island."

Detective Billie smiled. "Everything except beauty contests. Anita is a dyed-in-the-wool feminist when it comes to that kind of thing."

"Figures." Although I wouldn't attribute her motives to feminism. She preferred stories that "wrench your gut," as she so delicately put it. Not something as warm and fuzzy as the Mango Queen. Of course, now that a death had occurred, it was her kind of story—or, rather, Bernice's type of story.

"Anything else you want to tell me?" he said.

"Now that you ask . . . on the hike, I noticed that Gina's friend, Brandi, seemed a bit jealous. I mean, she *appeared* to be happy about Gina's being the Mango Queen, but I thought I detected a vibe. And I noticed that syringe near Gina's body. Do you think she was into drugs? Could her death have been an overdose or—"

"I'm going to stop you right there." Nick flipped his notebook shut. "*I'll* be investigating Gina's death, and you know I work *alone.*" He stressed the last word with pointed emphasis.

"Yes, but if you remember, I've helped you solve murder cases in the past, and—"

"No. You interfered in my cases and almost got yourself killed both times."

"That's not exactly true." I folded my arms across my rather flat chest. "You asked for my help at one point."

"Only to rescue a missing boy—not to apprehend his father's killer." His sharply planed features hardened. "Mallie, let me do my job."

"And I have to do mine. Bernice will want to make this a front-page story."

"That's fine. You stick to writing your stories, and I'll stick to law enforcement."

I heaved an exasperated sigh. Not so much at his implacable attitude, but because I found myself—in spite of my recent trauma—becoming aware of his tall, muscular shoulders and handsome face. I was okay when I didn't have to see him. But as soon as I was in his presence, my senses flared with an attraction as powerful as a wildfire.

"By the way, you're working on one heck of a sunburn," he commented.

"No kidding." I placed my palms on my cheeks. They felt warm—as well as sore and tender. *Jeez.* "I had no idea I'd be on the hike from hell when I set out this morning; otherwise, I would've slathered on my SPF 45. I'll probably have a few thousand new freckles from today."

"You need to be more careful." He fingered one of my curls.

My breath caught in my throat. "I thought you were still sort of irritated with me about that murder case last fall."

"When you barged into the elementary school to confront

the killer without waiting for me? Almost got yourself knifed? And jeopardized Madame Geri's life to boot?"

I lowered my head in guilt. "That would be the one."

"I'm over it—as long as you learned something." He dropped the curl, his fingers brushing my shoulder.

"I did, trust me." My head shot up again, a tiny jolt zinging through me. "Uh . . . when do you think you might know the cause of Gina's death?"

He paused. "In a few days."

"I'll drop by your office on Friday for an official statement—if that's okay."

"Agreed," he said, one side of his mouth turning up slightly. "By the way, don't mention the syringe to anyone. I don't want any rumors starting up before we have the facts." He took my hand and held it gently. "Are you okay?"

"Yeah . . . Nick." The word sounded odd coming out of my mouth, as if I was overstressing the last consonant.

We stood under that mammoth mangrove in awkward silence for few moments, hands touching. A death had taken place, and we had crossed a boundary.

Everything had changed.

I drove back to the *Observer* office and barely made it in the door before Sandy leaped out of her chair. "Is it true, Mallie? Is Gina the Mango Queen dead?"

My mouth dropped open. "How did you find out already? No, don't tell me. The Island Hardware store grapevine? Big Benny at the Circle K hotline?"

Sandy shook her head. "Neither. Miss Rose and Miss Emily from your Aunt Lily's quilting group were at Detective Billie's office reporting a stolen rocker—only it turns out it wasn't stolen. While Miss Rose was filing the paperwork, she remembered that she had taken it to the hardware store for the owner to paint. Anyway, they heard the news come over the police scanner in Nick's office. As soon as they picked up on Gina's name, they turned up their hearing aids and heard everything. Then they called your Aunt Lily, and she called here. She left you a message to call her cell phone." She handed me a small piece of paper. "She wants to meet you at the Seafood Shanty for lunch and—"

"What?" Had Sandy suddenly taken on my motormouth? Maybe all the ice cream had addled her brain.

"Which part didn't you get?"

I blinked. "Did my aunt really say she wanted to meet me at the Shanty?" Aunt Lily had sworn off that place months ago when a palmetto bug sashayed across her table and flipped itself into her iced tea.

"Yup." She leaned in closer and lowered her voice. "What really happened out there on the trail? What happened to Gina?"

I explained the sequence of events, ending with the last tragic scene under Old Blacky.

"So it could've been heatstroke or something," Sandy pondered aloud. "Speaking of which . . . uh . . . you're going to be peeling like a gumbo-limbo tree from that sunburn."

"I know. But that's not as bad as my poor feet." I raised one crusty shoe. "Not to mention that my Keds have turned into salt clodhoppers, thanks to Bernice's—"

"Did someone mention my name?" Bernice stood at the door to Anita's office, fiddling with her bracelets.

Anger bubbled up inside of me. "It would've been nice if you'd told me how long that stupid trail hike was, so I could've picked up my hat and sunblock."

"A little sun is good for you. Look at my skin—smooth and supple as a baby's bottom."

I tried not to recoil. She'd hit "bottom," all right. Her face, legs, and arms had the texture of a dried-up riverbed—cracked and shriveled.

"I heard you had some trouble?" A hopeful note entered Bernice's voice.

"Trouble?" I heaved my canvas bag onto my desk. "I guess you could call it that. We spent two hours of torture baking in the sun as we waded through the soggy wetlands, one of the hikers ended up dead, and I was the one who found the body. So I guess that qualifies as 'trouble.' "

"Dead?" She frowned, deepening the lines between her eyebrows. "Who was it?"

"Gina Fernandez, the Mango Queen."

"Oh, no! I was there when she was crowned." Bernice's body stiffened in shock. "I can't believe it."

Some of my anger dissolved at her reaction. Maybe she was more humane than the mean twin, Anita, after all.

"Hot damn! What an opportunity." She whipped out a new lollipop, her face kindling in excitement. " 'Terror on the Trail.' Yes, I love it. But I don't want a who, what, when, where thing. I want a juicy, first-person narrative. 'Mallie Meets Terror on the Trail'—that's even better. Talk about the hike—how you trudged through the swamp water, roasting in the sun. Then the emotion builds, and you relate how you found the body—a beautiful young woman cut down in the prime of her life. Bittersweet. Sad. All that kind of sentimental crap. And every step of the way, you'll delve into your deepest feelings. That's what people want to read about as you plumb the depths of human suffering. I want everyone to connect to your pain and—"

"I hardly knew Gina—not that I wasn't upset. But I can't say I'm . . . grieving," I protested. "Besides, this isn't a tabloid. We have to print the plain facts and unvarnished truth."

"Truth-schmuth." She waved a dismissive hand. "People want the nitty-gritty, and that's what we're going to give 'em."

Sandy made a choking sound and reached for her candy bar drawer.

"Bernice, we don't even know how Gina died. At this point, all we should do is print a story about her death and give some details about her life. More like an expanded obit."

"Boooooring! I want *reality* journalism." Bernice waved the lollipop in my face as if it were a weapon. "Look, Miss Priss, if you refuse to do it, I'll get someone in here who can. Writers for a rag like this are a dime a dozen."

I glared at her. She was *not* going to drive me out of my job. If I'd withstood the buffeting storms of Anita, I could ride out Bernice's turbulence too. I hadn't learned to stand up to challenges over the last year for nothing. Bernice was not going to find an excuse to fire me. "All right. But I refuse to write anything that could be considered libelous. I draw the line there." I folded my arms across my chest in defiance.

"Agreed." She weighed me with a critical squint. "Keep the sentimentality to a minimum, Miss Priss, and start writing that article—now. Chop-chop." She ducked back into Anita's office.

I turned my face toward the ceiling and gave a soundless scream. *Could the day turn any worse?*

Sandy handed me a large chocolate bar and started in on one herself. "Eat up," she urged. "It's the last resort of the downtrodden worker."

"I guess one won't hurt." I unwrapped the chocolate and bit into the creamy, thick food of the gods. "Did you find out where Anita went?"

She shook her head. "I checked her desk calendar, called her voice mail at her house, even stooped so low as to ask some of her neighbors. But no one seems to know—or care— where she's gone. Our last hope is Mr. Benton. I called his office, but he was out. His secretary didn't know anything, but she said he might have a vacation address that Anita left with him. So maybe he'll call this afternoon when he gets in. . . ."

"In the meantime, we'll have to cope with Butthead Bernice on our own." I finished off the chocolate bar, smacking my lips. "We've got to keep the *Observer* going with some semblance of journalistic integrity—if for nothing else than out of respect for Gina."

Sandy reached for her candy bar drawer again.

"No, Sandy." I seized her hand. "One bar only. You've got to be strong and not let Bernice get to you. Remember how long it took to reach your target weight on the diet? And how many times Anita drove you to distraction? Bernice isn't any worse than any of that. You *can't* give up now."

Sandy's lips trembled as she visibly fought temptation. "I'm not sure how long I can hold out. She's got me on the phone every hour with potential advertisers, including that creep, Fishin' Frank, who runs the Anchors Away nautical store."

"Not the guy who snaps out his fake eyeball and tosses it from hand to hand as he talks?"

"I'm afraid so."

I swallowed hard. He'd grossed out everyone at the last Town Hall meeting, including me, with a new trick: removing the glass eye and popping it into his mouth. The vision was burned into my memory. "Listen, Sandy, I know it seems bad, but chocolate won't help. It'll make you feel worse in the long run. You'll not only have to deal with Bernice, but you'll have to go back to wearing your clothes with the price tags tucked in so you can return them when your weight starts going up. You can't go back to those days." I didn't release her palm.

With a long sigh, Sandy withdrew her hand.

"That's more like it. I'll pick up an extra stock of Ozone Bars to keep you on track until this crisis is over."

She groaned. "I'm soooooo sick of those things."

"I know, but they work." I gave her a brief hug of encouragement. "Why don't you try Mr. Benton again?"

As she moved back to her desk, I reached for my phone and dialed Aunt Lily's cell.

She picked up on the first ring. "Mallie? I heard that you found Gina's body this morning. Are you okay?"

"Sort of." Visions of the Mango Queen's lovely face frozen in death rose up in my mind. I shivered and pushed the images away. "It was a real shocker. I mean, for her to die so suddenly like that—"

"It's worse than you think," Lily cut in with an urgency to her voice I'd never heard before. "I need to see you as soon as possible. I'm at the Seafood Shanty."

"Sandy already told me. Are you sure that you want to meet *there*?"

"I can't take a chance of running into anyone I know, because what I have to tell you is top secret."

My fingers tightened around the receiver. "Aunt Lily, what's wrong?"

She paused, and I could hear a loud male voice in the background, shouting an obscenity. Some biker wanting another brewsky?

"Hello? Aunt Lily?"

Her voice lowered to almost a whisper. "Gina's death was no accident. She was murdered."

I gasped, clutching the phone tighter. "Are you sure?"

"I'm sure."

"I'll be there in half an hour." Hanging up, I sat back in my chair. Was it possible? My aunt never lied, never exaggerated, never even embellished. If she said something was true, you could set your clock by it.

That meant one thing: a killer might be loose on Coral Island once again.

Chapter Three

Okay. In thirty minutes, I had to meet Aunt Lily at the Seafood Shanty. But how to make a quick exit?

I pretended to work on my story for a few minutes, while I formulated a plan to trick my temporary boss. I had to give Bernice what she wanted while secretly doing my own thing. She needed to think I was working on the "reality journalism" exposé of Gina's death. After a few minutes of mock "work," I rapped on the door to her cubicle, then swung it open.

"What?" she grumbled, her attention on her computer screen. "Bernice, I just got a call from a lead who might be ready to spill the beans about Gina's 'secret life.' "

Bernice turned away from the monitor and rubbed her hands together in glee. "What are you waiting for?"

I bit my lip in imitation distress. "But I thought you wanted me to work on the 'Terror on the Trail' piece—chop-chop."

"Chop-shmop." She waved a dismissive hand. "You'll have time to do that later. The important thing is to lock down that source. We want sleaze, sleaze, and more sleaze. The sleazier, the better. I want it so sleazy, you'll have to take a shower after you write the story. Readers don't want to know the good that people have done in their lives. They want to know about secret marriages, illegitimate children, and eating disorders—in no particular order," she hastened to add.

"If you insist," I tossed in with mock reluctance as I backed out of her office. Before she could change her mind, I shut down my computer and made for the door, flashing Sandy a double thumbs-up. I'd won this skirmish through lies and subterfuge. That aging, tackily dressed old bag was no match for Mallie Monroe.

"Don't be gone too long, okay?" Sandy pleaded.

"I won't. If you promise not to have any more candy bars."

She held up two chocolate-stained fingers. "Girl Scout's honor."

"Were you a Girl Scout?"

"No."

"It's still an oath."

She managed a brave facsimile of a smile. "Don't forget to take those tennis shoes off. I think your feet are turning to stone."

"Ohmygod, I forgot." I managed to pry the salt-ridden Keds off my feet and don a pair of beachy flip-flops that I kept at the office. *At least I could curl my toes again.* I breezed out of the office, into the blazing midday sun. Covering my scorched face from the sun with my hands, I dashed for Rusty and drove off.

I arrived at the Seafood Shanty within the time I'd promised my great-aunt. As I pulled into the parking lot, I scanned the vehicles. Big black Harleys mixed with beat-up trucks—the usual patrons, then. Aunt Lily would stick out like the proverbial sore thumb.

I entered the shabby building, taking a few moments for my eyes to adjust to the dim light. As the room came into focus, I beheld the fish netting hanging from the low ceiling, the long bar at one end with leather-clad bikers seated on the stools, and the dirty floor littered with empty peanut shells. *Classy place all around.*

Off at a corner table sat my great-aunt, Lily, like a beacon of feminine refinement. She wore a simple lavender silk blouse, gauzy skirt, and silver sandals. As I drew closer, I noticed that she wore large, oval-shaped sunglasses and hid the lower half of her face behind a menu.

"Aunt Lily? Are you okay?"

"Sit," she instructed as she pushed a menu in front of me. "Open it, and keep your head down."

I did as she requested, taking a furtive glance around the room. "I don't think you have to worry about being seen— unless you've been dating some Harley guys on the side."

"Not likely." She removed the sunglasses. Red-rimmed eyes fastened on me.

"Aunt Lily, have you been crying?" Now I really was concerned, because I'd never seen my great-aunt cry on any occasion. Not at Christmas when we sang sentimental carols. Not at Valentine's Day when we read Hallmark cards at the drugstore. Not even at a sentimental "chick flick," when I was reduced to a blubbering mass of tears at some couple separated by time, space, or inability to work a cheese dip together. Okay, maybe the last one was pushing it. "Auntie?"

"I've been a little . . . teary-eyed, I guess," she admitted.

"A lot."

"Guess so." She scanned my face. "Oh, Mallie, what happened to your skin?"

"Forget that for now. What was your call all about?" I leaned in closer. "Did you know Gina?"

She sniffed, and her eyes turned watery. "Since she was a baby. I've been friends with her mother even longer than that."

"I'm so sorry." I reached for her hand. Her smooth but icy-cold fingers locked around my palm.

"My loss is nothing compared to her mother's—Mama Maria's."

"That's her mom? The woman who runs the Mexican restaurant by the same name?"

She nodded. "Mama Maria Fernandez."

"Ohmygod. I've been in Mama Maria's place a hundred times for the chicken quesadillas and never saw Gina there. But every so often I had the beef tortilla—it was just as good." I paused. "Okay . . . sorry to get off topic. I had no idea she was Gina's mother. She doesn't look . . . uh . . . old enough to have a grown daughter." I broke off, not wanting to sound insensitive. Mama Maria was about six inches shorter than Gina and about ten inches wider.

"You didn't know Maria when she was young. She was very pretty."

I guess my true meaning hadn't escaped her.

"I'm sure," I said in a soft voice. Then a blast of country-western music filled the room. I couldn't identify the singer, but he was wailing about the usual triad: missed trains, lost love, and unfaithful women. "Have you talked to Mama Maria?"

"About an hour ago. She was so upset, she could hardly speak."

"What about Gina's dad?"

She stiffened. "He's been out of the picture for a long time."

"Was Gina her only child?"

"She's got a son, Rivas. He's seventeen and hot-tempered to boot. That's the main reason I called you." She took in a deep breath and caught my gaze with her tortured eyes. "I want you to find Gina's killer. You need to get him before Rivas does. I don't want Mama Maria to lose both of her children."

"Whoa. Wait a minute. Let's back up." I folded my menu

and set it on the table. "I don't know for sure how Gina died. Detective Billie won't have that information until Friday. And even if it turns out to be murder, I can't just go tracking down her killer. If I interfere with one of Nick Billie's investigations again, he'll lock me up for sure." *Not to mention, he'd nix the hand-holding.*

"I'll help you, I promise."

"That's nice, but I don't think you can—"

"Hey, Mallie, is that you, babe?" Nora Cresswell approached us, her baby boy nestled in one of those slings across her chest.

"Hi." I pasted a smile onto my face. "I thought you weren't waitressing here anymore."

"I'm not. The owner hired me to do the books, since I finished my accounting course." Her eyes widened in surprise as she noticed the identity of my companion. "Miss Lily? What are you doing here?"

Lily shut her menu and pasted an identical smile onto her face. "Mallie finally convinced me to try the cheeseburger. I love a good burger—yum."

Nora's forehead crinkled in confusion as she patted her son's back. "You do?"

"Oh, yes. Quarter pound of meat smothered in lettuce, ketchup, and pickles. My mouth's watering just talking about it." She smacked her lips.

"Well, in that case, let me order some up for you gals." She motioned a young girl over who sported a ponytail, miniskirt, and heavy makeup. "Patsy, these are my friends, and they'd each like a cheeseburger—with the works."

"Fries?" Patsy snapped her gum.

"Why not?" Aunt Lily said with a wave of her hand.

Pasty scribbled a few words onto her order pad and strolled off. When she reached the bar, she turned and shouted, "Whaddya both want to drink?"

Two of the bikers swiveled on their stools, grinning with interest.

"Two unsweetened iced teas," I yelled back.

The bikers immediately lost interest. I guess they only hit on women who drank sweetened tea—or something even stronger.

"Will do!" Patsy gave a little salute with her pen.

Nora gritted her teeth, adjusting her son to the other side. "It's so hard to get decent wait staff these days. The owner has been training that ditz, Patsy, for almost a month, and she still bellows out the orders like she's doing cattle calls."

"You'll get her to tone it down," I assured her. "How's little Josh doing?" I rubbed her son's soft, wispy blond hair.

"Sweet as a spring breeze—and full of joy." Her face brightened into a sunny glow as she dropped a kiss onto his head. "Not that life runs real smooth anymore. Let me tell ya, he can put up a fuss like you wouldn't believe. But Pete is such a patient dad, it makes the whole thing a lot easier."

"Josh is a lucky little guy to have two great parents." I shook his tiny hand, remembering how different Nora had looked when I first met her. Separated from Pete at the time, she'd worn the weary, tense look of a woman who'd turned down a wrong road and couldn't find her way back. It took Pete's being arrested for a murder he hadn't committed to shock her into remembering how much she loved her husband. Today, Nora's eyes beamed with happiness and contentment.

"*We're* the lucky ones," she enthused. Then her gaze fastened on my great-aunt. "Miss Lily, you're mighty quiet."

"Just old age, my dear." My aunt averted her face. "It's nothing."

"I wouldn't call it *nothing*," I cut in. "Nora's a friend, and I think you should tell her the truth."

"What? Has something happened?" Nora's arms instinctively closed around her baby.

"It's Gina Fer . . . Fernandez." Aunt Lily managed to sputter the name. "She's . . . uh . . . I can't say it." A tear spilled down the faded freckles on her cheek.

"She died this morning," I said in a quiet voice.

"Gina!" Nora's arms tightened around Josh in protection. "I can't believe it. She was just crowned Mango Queen. And now she's . . . gone? What? How?"

"We don't know yet." I shook my head. "She was found under a mangrove tree near the start of the Little Coral Island trail."

"Who found her?"

Aunt Lily extended an index finger toward me.

"Oh, Mallie, not again," Nora protested. Just then, Josh began to whimper, and she slipped a pacifier into his mouth. "You're like some kind of magnet for bad events."

"Just call me Mishap Mallie," I quipped. "It must rub off from working at the *Observer* with one crazy boss after another."

Nora gave me a rueful smile, then turned serious again as she asked Aunt Lily, "How's Mama Maria taking it?"

"Not well," Aunt Lily said.

"Please let her know how sorry I am about her daughter. I know some island folk didn't like Gina, but she was always nice to me and Pete."

My attention spiked. "Who didn't like her?"

Patsy brought our burgers and iced teas, suspending the conversation for a few minutes.

"Well . . . maybe I shouldn't say this," Nora began, "but her prospective in-laws for starters—Bryan and Trish Palmer. They never accepted Gina's engagement last year to their son, Brett. If you ask me, those people are too stuck-up for their own good." Josh's whimpering continued, and Nora adjusted his pacifier. "Their daughter, Brandi, pretended to be Gina's friend, but—"

"Brandi is Brett's sister?" I cut in, surprised.

Nora nodded. "But she's nothing like him. If looks could've killed a couple of nights ago, she would've struck Gina dead to get the Mango Queen title."

"Really?" *I thought I'd detected a vibe!*

Nora rolled her eyes. "Absolutely. You have no idea how important Mango Queen is on Coral Island—it's like the highest honor, and the contestants are *very* cutthroat. Women campaign all year to win the title. Usually it's someone from the old families—the ones who originally homesteaded on the island—"

"And Gina was an upstart?" I finished for her.

"Not in that kind of way. Her family has been on the island since the turn of the century—but from the wrong side of the tracks. Her grandfather was a migrant worker."

Aunt Lily gave an exclamation of disgust. "I can't believe that people think like that in this day and age. It's positively medieval."

"I'm not saying *I* agree," Nora continued. "Heck, I grew up poor, and we're not exactly on the Coral Island social list right now. But I understand how some folks can get all revved up about feeling important. If it meant that much to Gina to be Mango Queen, as far as I'm concerned, she was welcome to it."

"Now the title will go to Brandi," I mused aloud.

"Ain't that just convenient as all get-out?" Nora pursed her mouth. "Was there something . . . fishy about her death?"

I hesitated. "Not so far."

"Which means you're suspicious." Nora opened her mouth to continue, but Josh decided to make his presence known by spitting out the pacifier and wailing at the top of his lungs.

"Sorry, gals, it's time for his feeding. Let me know if you find out anything else about Gina's death. And please tell Mama Maria I'm thinking about her if you see her."

"I will." Aunt Lily gave a quick nod.

I waited until Nora had exited before I turned to my great-aunt. "Okay, is that why you think Gina was murdered? Because she had a bunch of snooty future in-laws who didn't like her?"

"Sort of." Her lined face suddenly sagged with every one of her seventy-five years. "Gina refused to accept that she was supposed to be a second-class citizen on the island because her family came from migrant workers. That earned her some enemies. . . ."

"But everyone goes to Mama Maria's—it's a landmark. Why would people treat her daughter like dirt?"

"Oh, sure, they'll go to Maria's restaurant, eat her food, and enjoy her hospitality. But when it comes to her daughter breaking into the ranks of Coral Island society, that's another matter. Gina ran a successful interior-design company, was engaged to the island's most eligible bachelor, and made Mango Queen. Her very success was a kick in the face to island snobs."

"Still, that doesn't mean someone killed her."

"Then how do you explain a young woman, in the prime of her life, ending up dead for no apparent reason?" Lily thumped her arms on the table with anger and frustration. Unfortunately, our glasses had been filled to the brim, and the action ended up splashing iced tea across the table.

I took my napkin and sopped up the mess.

"I'm only proposing that you ask around, see if you can dig up any information that might show whether or not Gina was murdered. That's your job, after all. You're an investigative journalist." Lily wiped her arms with her napkin.

"I'm not so sure Bernice would agree with you. She's running the show until Anita returns, and all she wants is some kind of sensationalized exposé on Gina's life."

"When is Anita coming back?"

"I don't know—maybe a week. Sandy and I are trying to find out where she went, but it's as if she fell off the face of the earth. I still can't believe she put Butthead Bernice in charge."

"That's Anita for you. She's always done things her own way." Aunt Lily folded her napkin and lay it on the table. "Just talk to Mama Maria. Please, Mallie."

"How could I ever say no to you?" I gave her a quick pat. "Besides, I'd like to know the truth."

She sat back in her rickety wooden chair. "Good enough."

I picked up my hamburger, dripping in grease. "Now, dig in."

"Oh, dear." Dismay touched Aunt Lily's face. "Do I actually have to eat this thing?"

"It's the price you pay for going incognito." I took a large bite out of my own burned beef on a bun. "Dig in."

"All right." Lily slipped her fingers around the burger and raised it to her mouth. "But I don't have to like it."

Someone spiked the volume on the country-western music even higher. We abandoned trying to talk over the throbbing steel guitar and finished our lunches in silence. There was nothing else to say. She had piqued my curiosity, and she knew it. I wanted to know what had happened to Gina Fernandez.

A little while later, I pulled up in front of Mama Maria's restaurant. A small stuccoed building neatly painted white with yellow shutters, it stood to one side of Cypress Road—the island's main drag.

Mama Maria's late-model Buick occupied the normally crowded parking lot. A serviceable vehicle. Midsized, mid-priced, mid-everything. And all alone. It spoke volumes.

As did the empty parking lot.

Word of Gina's death must've gotten around most of the island by now.

I slapped another layer of aloe lotion onto my throbbing, sunburned nose and then headed for the entrance. Potted palms and dwarf hibiscus bushes graced either side of the front screen door. A CLOSED sign with a frowning Disney character greeted me. *Yikes.*

Hesitating for a few seconds, I knocked.

No answer.

I banged on the door with more force. "Mama Maria? Are you in there?" Raising my hand to shield my eyes, I strained to see into the small restaurant. All I could make out were empty tables. It felt sad, forlorn.

"Hello!" I shouted.

A muffled voice responded, but I couldn't make out what it said.

"It's Mallie Monroe. My Aunt Lily asked me to come over and talk to you. She's very concerned." Growing a bit alarmed, I swung open the screen door and glanced around the homey dining room. A dozen or so tables were set with linen cloths and silver flatware. But no mouthwatering smells assailed my senses. The whole place felt deserted, like a ghost town built on a dream that had come and gone. I shuddered.

All of a sudden, the sound of breaking glass and a muttered curse came out of the kitchen.

"Mama Maria?" I crept toward the kitchen.

"Madre de dios." Another sound of shattering glass echoed through the restaurant.

I tiptoed into the kitchen—no small feat with flip-flops snapping like elastic bands with every step.

Mama Maria stood in front of a large chopping block, a

crystal goblet in each hand. She raised each hand high and slammed the glasses onto the tile floor. They smashed into hundreds of jagged pieces. From the amount of broken glass on the floor, it looked as if she'd been at it for quite some time.

"Hi, it's Mallie Monroe," I repeated.

She looked up at me with unseeing eyes.

"Remember me? I've been in with my great-aunt, Lily, several times. We had the vegetarian tacos last week, with refried beans, a side salad, and iced tea. I meant to tell you, it was a fabulous meal. I had to stagger out to Rusty—that's my truck. I named him on account of the rust. Of course, you wouldn't care about that, and I don't blame you. What with everything that has happened. I'm just so sorry about Gina. I only met her today, but she was beautiful—and not just on the outside. She must've really been quite a remarkable person to make Mango Queen. . . ." Okay, I was at it again. Motormouth extraordinaire babbling on and on. But the sight of Mama Maria, defeated and desperate in her kitchen, wrung out my heart. I didn't know what to say, so I said everything.

"She was the light of my life. The kind of daughter every mother would want. My poor *chica*." Tears rolled down her cheeks. "I can't believe she's gone. How can that be?"

"I don't know."

She picked up two more goblets. "These were engagement gifts—Gina's favorite pattern: Crystal Fantasy. She said they reminded her of how blessed her life was since she'd become engaged to Brett." Mama Maria smashed them against the floor. "It isn't a dream any longer. More like a nightmare." Her head drooped to her chest.

I carefully threaded my way across the glass-strewn floor. When I reached Mama Maria, she threw her arms around my neck and sagged against me, sobbing. I let her cry. As the torrent of tears fell, her stout body shook as if she were buffeted by a strong wind. I don't know how long we stood there, but eventually she raised her head and took in a deep breath.

"Forgive me for letting myself go like that," she said in a shaky voice, smoothing down her dark hair.

"There's nothing to forgive." I led her to a chair and knelt down. "All of this must be quite a shock to you."

"*Sí.*" She pushed the dark cloud of hair back from her face. "When Nick Billie called me, I thought there must've been a mistake. He had the wrong girl. But, no, it was Gina. My sweet Gina." She pulled out a white lace handkerchief and dabbed at her eyes. "I was getting ready to prepare chicken fajitas for the lunch crowd, and—"

Without warning, the back door was flung open. A young man with mussed, wiry hair and wild eyes appeared.

He held a gun in his right hand.

Chapter Four

What are you doing?" Mama Maria jumped to her feet as she spied the intruder. "Have you gone *loco*?"

"Don't try to stop me." He waved the gun over his head.

Jeez! I crouched down even farther.

"Rivas, put that away," she ordered, "before you do something stupid like blast a hole in the roof."

My eyes widened. *How about shoot a* person?

"It's only a water gun, Mama." He slowly lowered it and looked in my direction. "Is this the gringa from the *Observer* who found my sister?"

"Uh . . . that would be me." I rose to my feet, my knees shaking. The water gun sure looked real enough to me. "You know, you scared the heck out of me."

"So sorry, Mallie. This is my *estúpido* son, Rivas," Mama Maria explained.

"Do you know what happened to Gina?" He moved toward me, the water gun still in his hand.

"We're not sure." I kept a wary eye on him. Even if the gun was a fake, his anger was real. "When I found her, she was

45

already d . . . deceased under a mangrove tree. The island's chief deputy, Detective Billie, said he'd have the . . . cause of death by the end of the week."

With his free hand, Rivas rubbed his forehead and moaned. "I knew something was gonna happen to her."

"What do you mean?" I asked.

"She didn't know her place. My poor sister always wanted more. And she tried to mix with gringos who always looked down on her no matter what she did."

Mama Maria bristled. "That's not true."

"Of course it is, Mama. Oh, they'd come in here and tell you how *bonita* your daughter is, but our worlds are separate. Gina was the only person who didn't know that. . . ."

"But I thought she was engaged to Brett Palmer," I said.

Rivas gave an exclamation of disgust. "They never would've married. His family didn't accept her. And now they've killed her."

"Rivas!" Mama Maria placed both hands on her hips. "*Silencio.* You are talking like a fool."

"Am I?" He yanked a hand through his tousled hair.

"Did anyone from her fiancé's family make threatening remarks to Gina?" I inquired.

Rivas shook his head. "They didn't have to. I could see the hatred in their eyes. Especially the parents. They went along with the engagement, but they were always plotting to split them up." He spat on the glass-strewn floor. "Now that my sister is permanently out of the picture, they're probably throwing a fiesta."

"Get a hold of yourself," Mama Maria demanded.

"But—"

"And give me that water gun—it looks too real. Someone could mistake it and think you were dangerous, not just foolish—*comprende?*" Her voice grew strong, and she straightened her shoulders. "I've already lost one child. Do you think I want to lose another one because you let that temper of yours lead you into doing something even more *loco*?"

I held my breath, not sure which one would give in first. Finally, Rivas shuffled toward his mother and gave her the water gun.

I let out a long sigh of relief. Even though it was fake, it still unnerved me.

"Son, promise me that you won't do or say anything until we know how Gina died," Mama Maria said.

Rivas touched two fingers to his heart, then held them up. "I swear."

"And no more guns."

"*Sí.*"

Mama Maria slipped the phony firearm into her dress pocket. "Now that that's taken care of, I can mourn my daughter without worrying myself sick over my son."

Rivas muttered a Spanish expletive and slammed out of the room.

"I'm sorry you had to see that, but my son is . . . grieving." Mama Maria opened a cupboard and deposited the water gun into a large ceramic bowl.

"Grief can make people do crazy things. I know when my Aunt Phoebe, on my father's side, choked to death on a chicken bone, my cousins couldn't even look at any type of poultry for years. I think they've relented and have turkey on Thanksgiving now, but it's the boneless frozen roast that looks like a lump of processed goop in a tinfoil pan." Okay, so I was at it again. This whole intense scene was causing my motormouth to lock into high gear. And I was talking nonsense, to boot. *Oh, joy.* Just what Mama Maria needed right now. A blabbing idiot. "Of course, there's nothing wrong with chicken. . . . I wasn't trying to impugn your chicken fajitas."

Surprisingly, Mama Maria just stared at me—then she gave a short laugh. "Lily always said you could talk the scales off of a *pescado*—fish. I didn't know what she meant—until now."

"I think it's genetic—like a harelip or something."

"Not nearly so bad." She shrugged. "I needed a moment of . . . lightness."

"If there's anything I can do to help you, please let me know." I gave her one of my *Observer* business cards. The woman was suffering, and I just couldn't press her for details about her daughter right now. "I'd like to drop by later this week and get some information about Gina for the newspaper, if that's okay."

"You mean her obituary?"

I gulped. "Yes."

"Come *mañana*." Mama Maria stood there for a few moments, reviewing the mess she'd created in the kitchen. "I've got to clean up now—I guess I, too, went a little *loco*. But breaking glasses won't bring my Gina back." She reached for the plastic broom in a corner. "Tell Lily I'll call her later."

Watching her rhythmically sweep the floor, I marveled at her strength. Then I let myself out the back door, only to find Rivas leaning against a palm tree trunk, smoking the last of a cigarette. He flicked the stub to the sandy ground and crushed it under his heel.

"I wanted to talk to you, *chica*."

I edged around him. "I've got to get back to the *Observer*." And away from this water gun–toting wild man.

He hooked his thumbs into the waist of his jeans. "I know I must've seemed *loco* in there. But I'd just heard Gina was dead—it hurts so bad." He took in a long, deep breath. "You know, the kind of pain that hits right in the gut. I'm sorry if I scared you." The stricken expression on his face halted me.

"I . . . I guess I sort of understand. She was your sister, after all." Still, I kept a healthy distance between us. "What did you want to tell me?"

"I wasn't lying when I said Brett Palmer's family hated Gina. They would've done anything to get rid of my sister."

"Even kill her?"

"Sí." His mouth turned mutinous. "I overheard Brett's parents talking at the engagement party. They said the marriage would never take place—they'd make sure of it—no matter what."

"They may not have wanted Gina as part of the family, but that doesn't mean they killed her. Sometimes people just say things." *And think them.* I refrained from telling him that I'd frequently contemplated all sorts of ways to avoid every family gathering my mother had planned over the years—including the annual family reunion picnic in the Midwest. Every one was the same: sour lemonade, dry ham, and overachieving siblings. *Ugh.*

Rivas mumbled something in Spanish under his breath. "The Palmers were serious."

"Well . . ."

"You're a reporter. It's your job to ask people questions." He weighed me with a critical squint. "You can find out if they did something to harm my sister."

"That's not exactly what I do, you—"

"Gina's dead!" He thumped his chest with his fists. "Her soul won't rest until I find out what happened to her."

"You might want to talk to Detective Billie. He's conducting the investigation."

"Police. Bah." He ground the cigarette butt farther into the ground. "They do nothing to help the island workers."

I hesitated.

"Please. You *must* help us." His eyes had a tortured sadness in the depths that tugged at my heart.

Mentally kicking myself, I reached into my cavernous canvas

bag and pulled out my notepad. "Give me the address of Brett's parents."

"They live in *muy elegante* Sea Belle Isle Point—1565 Hibiscus Court. That's where they had the engagement party."

"Is there anyone else I could talk to about Gina?"

"Her partner, Isabel. They ran a decorating business together called Island Décor."

"Oh, yeah, I know where that is—near the island center." Needless to say, I'd never set foot inside. One could only do so much with an Airstream trailer like the one I lived in. The furniture was built into the unit, and I'd fixed it up with my version of shabby chic—heavy on the shabby, light on the chic. "I'll see what I can dig up, but I can't make you any promises."

"*Gracias.* I won't forget this." He gave a brief nod and went back inside Mama Maria's restaurant.

I flipped my notepad shut. Something told me I was getting myself into a big, messy muddle. But what could I do? Aunt Lily had begged me to find out what happened to Gina. Now Rivas Fernandez was doing the same thing. And both of them thought there was something suspicious about Gina's demise.

Where there's smoke, there's fire—or at least there might *be.*

Certainly I was becoming more and more intrigued that people *thought* Gina's death seemed suspicious.

I drove toward the island center, passed the *Observer* office, and stopped at the suite of offices near the four-way stop that led off the island. Unlike the tiny, ground-level strip mall that housed our newspaper office, this structure was up four feet on concrete blocks, fashioned in a quad of offices, with latticework along the bottom and a sparkling new tin roof.

It had that "old Florida" look that was hot right now. But with plastic siding, plastic porch rails, and plastic shutters, it was *old* as in the *Neo-Plastic Era.*

I located the Island Décor suite and swung open the door, causing a tiny chime to tinkle somewhere in the back. Inhaling the sickly sweet odor of a vanilla candle, I grimaced and took stock of the place. Plush carpet, expensive knickknacks, and an antique desk graced the room, along with a wall filled with paint chips and fabric-swatch catalogues. *Swanky decorators.* Not that *I* had ever consulted them, but my mother was a frequent purveyor of decorating experts. She liked to call it "having the house *done.*" Luckily, I never had to bother with paint choices—Airstreams came in three basic colors: silver, silver, and silver. Period.

"May I help you?" a young woman asked. She looked to be about Gina's age but much taller. Dark hair with deep gold highlights and hazel eyes. Quite striking.

"Are you Gina Fernandez's partner?"

"Yes. I'm Isabel Morales. We co-own Island Décor." She shook hands with me. "We offer a full range of services that cover all aspects of decorating, from soup to nuts." She laughed at her little metaphor. "You name it, we can do it. Gina and I have decorated some of the finest homes on Coral Island, and I mean the ritzy mansions on Sea Belle Isle Point."

"I get the drift." Translated: Unless kidnapped by decorating terrorists, she wouldn't even drive into the Twin Palms RV Resort where my Airstream currently resided. No big money there.

She picked up a clipboard and handed it to me. "Here is the questionnaire that we have all our clients fill out. I need to know what your color preferences are, what type of furniture you prefer—modern or traditional—what your decorating budget allows, and—"

"I live in a trailer."

"Oh." She snatched the clipboard back.

Guess that was the deal breaker. "Well, I'm not here for

decorating advice anyway," I said, noting the haughty tilt her head had assumed. "I'd like to talk about Gina."

"She won't be in until tomorrow. She had some sort of trail hike to do this morning and was going to spend the afternoon shopping with her fiancé, Brett." Her lip curled as she said his name. "If you want, I can take down your phone number and—"

"You mean you haven't heard?" Was it possible I'd finally met someone *not* plugged into the island gossip grapevine? *Oh, dear.*

"Heard what?"

I paused. "You might want to sit down."

Her eyes widened in alarm as she sank into an overstuffed, flowered-chintz sofa.

"Gina . . . uh . . . died today."

"But . . . no, that can't be." Her hands tightened around the armrest until her knuckles turned white. "She was fine this morning when we had coffee at Mama Maria's. I don't understand."

"The cause of death is still undetermined, but she was found under a mangrove tree near the entrance to the Little Coral Island Trail."

"Madre de dios." She crossed herself, the haughty demeanor falling away as if it were a discarded piece of clothing. "She didn't even want to go on that stupid trail hike, but Brandi insisted. Said it was her first official duty as Mango Queen."

"I know you're probably upset, but let me try to reconstruct what you know." I reached into my cavernous canvas bag and pulled out my notepad. "You had coffee this morning at Mama Maria's with Gina and Brandi. Then they left to hike the trail, and you came here to work."

"Yes. We had a big job to finish—her prospective in-laws' house. I was having trouble with the bathroom vanities. Trish

Palmer wanted them raised five inches higher than standard, but it was hard to find a carpenter to do it within the time frame she wanted for completion. So I was on the phone all morning. Then I had to drive onto the mainland to pick up these special gold faucets for the master bath." Her mouth trembled. "I just got in this minute."

"And I had to be the one to give you the bad news." I cleared my throat. "So sorry."

Tears welled up in her eyes. "Why are you so interested in Gina?"

"I work for the *Observer*—Mallie Monroe. I'm writing a story on Gina, about her life and sudden death." No need to tell her that I'd found the body—or seen that syringe. "People on Coral Island will want to know what happened to their Mango Queen."

Isabel buried her head in her hands and emitted a sound somewhere between a sob and a groan. "That stupid contest. I don't know why she was so obsessed with being Mango Queen." She raised her head, tears streaking mascara down her cheeks in long black tracks. "She spent months and months learning about the island's history and the mango industry— all so she could claim the title and impress Brett's parents."

"They must've respected her if they hired her to decorate their house."

She gave a scornful laugh. " 'Hired help' is a far cry from daughter-in-law. We're good enough to decorate their house, but not to live in it. They tolerated Gina's engagement to Brett, but I don't think they'll be mourning at her funeral." Her tone had turned bitter.

"She and Brandi seemed to be friends."

"No way." Isabel wiped her cheeks with the back of one hand. "Brandi *pretended* to like Gina because of Brett. They've always been a close brother and sister. But make no mistake, Brandi wanted to be Mango Queen by hook or by crook. She was seething with envy this morning when Gina walked into Mama Maria's wearing her Mango Queen crown."

"Huh?" I stopped scribbling. "Was it made of . . . mangos?"

"No, of course not. It was a tiara, like the beauty queens wear."

This Mango Queen thing *was* big. A tiara? On Coral Island, where most of the population rarely wore shoes? "So you think Brandi might've wanted to see Gina out of the way so she could be the Mango Queen?"

Isabel blinked a couple of times. "Wait a minute. How did Gina die? Is there something suspicious about her death?"

"I can't say for sure. As I told you, it's undetermined."

"But you're asking a lot of questions."

"That's my job." At least it was when I left the office that morning. Who knew what changes Bernice had made since then?

"This is just . . . unbelievable. Gina was my friend and partner." She gazed up at me with desperation. "What's going to happen to our decorating business? I can't run the company on my own. Gina was the one who brought the clients in. . . ." She broke off, staring into the distance as if she could see a bleak, dismal future.

The door chime rang, and I looked over at the entrance. A thin, middle-aged guy with a ferretlike face stood there. He wore a slate-gray suit and loafers—formal dress indeed for the island. "Hi, Isabel."

"I just lost my business partner—Gina," she sobbed.

Shock registered on his pinched features. "Oh, I'm so sorry. I just saw her a few nights ago when she was elected Mango Queen. She died?"

"Yes." I spoke up. "I'm Mallie Monroe from the *Observer*, and I'm writing her obituary—that's why I'm here." *Sort of true.*

"Homer Finch—my law office is next door." He blinked several times in rapid succession. "I didn't know her very well, but she was lovely."

Isabel nodded mutely.

"If there's anything I can do, let me know," he said to Isabel. He stood there in awkward silence for a few moments and then exited.

I turned back to Isabel. "Can you give me any more information on Gina?"

"Here's the brochure we give to potential clients. It has a short bio on each of us."

I flipped open the glossy white document. Pictures of Gina and Isabel dominated it, each posing on various lushly colored pieces of furniture. "Distinctive photos."

"They were Gina's idea. She always said that first impressions count."

"Thanks." I gave her one of my cards. "Call me if you have anything else you want to pass on."

She gave a brief nod.

I exited Island Décor to the tune of the tinkling chime. I hadn't found out much, except that, as I'd suspected that morning, Brandi might've been pretending to be Gina's best friend. Apparently she *had* coveted the Mango Queen crown.

Enough to want to kill Gina?

It was late afternoon by the time I returned to the *Observer* office. For a few minutes, I stood outside the door in the suffocating heat and humidity, preparing myself for whatever unpleasantness would greet me once I entered. The words that Dante wrote about hell in the *The Divine Comedy* came to mind: *Abandon hope, all ye who enter here.*

I tossed my curls in defiance and pushed open the door. This was no time to let my comparative-literature imagination run away with me. Maybe this wasn't paradise, but it wasn't exactly the inferno, either.

Not yet.

The first thing I noticed was the smell. *Uh-oh.* The standard office aroma usually contained a combination of odors from Sandy's burned low-fat popcorn, burned snacks, and burned coffee. But a new, strange scent permeated the air. I sniffed, trying to pinpoint it: fish. Raw fish.

I looked at Sandy. She sported a miserable expression and a too-tight T-shirt that read *Hooked on Bait.* Next to her desk sat a large white cooler with the lid flung open.

"What's going on?" I approached her desk, and the fish smell grew stronger.

"Bernice's new idea. Advertisers with the paper get to display their products here—she thinks we get enough foot traffic from people coming in to pay for their subscriptions to make it worthwhile. Danny from the Bait Shack bought a quarter-page ad, so Bernice said he could keep some of his best shrimp bait here for people to sample." She pinched her nostrils and groaned. "I've never had to smell something so vile. What's more, she's got me wearing this hideous, too-small T-shirt." She pulled out the sides, but the thin cotton fabric snapped back and outlined every generous curve. "I ate two more candy bars since the cooler arrived, and I can't seem to stop. If I keep going at this rate, everything I own will be too small pretty soon. I'll be back to shopping plus women's sizes, and—"

"Sandy, calm down. That's not going to happen."

She released her nose, then wrinkled it again as the odor penetrated her nostrils. "It's just so humiliating to sit here next to shrimp bait. This is an *office,* for goodness' sake."

"At least it used to be," I quipped, trying not to step too close to the offensive source of the fishy smell. "Did you find out anything yet on Anita's whereabouts?"

"Nope. And now Mr. Benton seems to have gone AWOL too. His secretary called back and said he took a sudden out-of-town trip."

"Benton?" I frowned. "He never leaves town. He's worse than Anita about taking vacations—too cheap for even a bus trip."

"I know. Just when we need him, he takes off too."

"Keep trying Anita's voice mail—at home and on her cell phone. She's got to check her messages sometime."

"Do you think if I just left a scream on both, it would sound too desperate?"

Inhaling the fish bait again, I staggered slightly. "Go for it."

Sandy started to punch in Anita's number, then paused. "What did you find out about Gina?"

"Nothing concrete." *True enough.* Everyone I'd talked to today had given me only speculations as to the cause of Gina's death. I mentally reviewed the list. Aunt Lily thought Brandi did Gina in for the Mango Queen title. Gina's partner, Isabel, agreed. Gina's brother, Rivas, however, thought Brett's parents had gotten rid of her so their precious son could find a more suitable bride. All were plausible.

"Poor Gina," Sandy commented.

"I did learn a couple of things: I had no idea the Mango Queen thing was such a big deal or that Coral Island has its own snobby social scene." I plopped my canvas bag onto my desk.

"A lot of people didn't like that Gina was elected Mango Queen," Sandy concurred. "You haven't been here all that long, but I grew up on this island, and I'm telling you, there's a class pyramid here just like everywhere else. At the top are the wealthy people at Sea Belle Isle Point; then you've got the middle class like Jimmy and me; then the fishermen who barely eke out a living; and at the bottom are the migrant workers. Gina's family raised their position a little when Mama Maria opened the restaurant, but everyone remembers that Gina's grandfather picked mangos for a living."

"I can't believe that would matter in this day and age—"

"To a snooty family from Sea Belle Isle Point?" she asked, her eyebrows rising. "You'd better believe it matters."

"What matters?" Butthead Bernice appeared in the doorway to "her" office.

"Nothing," I muttered as I switched on my computer. "Turns out my lead didn't know anything about Gina's 'secret life.' "

"You wasted a whole afternoon and got nothing?" She placed both chubby hands on her hips.

I swiveled my crooked wooden chair around and faced her with a bland expression. "Sometimes journalism is like that. You track down leads that go nowhere. Anita would understand."

"My sister is an idiot. I intend to get the lowdown on Gina. In the meantime . . ." She reached into her office for something. "I know how to turn a buck. In fact, I just landed another advertiser myself. Here." She handed me a white T-shirt.

"I refuse to promote the Bait Shack."

"You don't have to." A grin overtook her features. "I said I just landed another advertiser."

I held up the shirt. Blazoned across the front were the words *Feast with Me at the Frozen Flamingo.* A large pink flamingo curved around the slogan, holding an ice cream cone in one of its claws.

My heart sank.

Chapter Five

I didn't have the energy to argue with her. I just grabbed the offensive T-shirt and made a quick exit, mumbling something about working on my story at home. Of course, I had no intention of doing that, but I had to get out of that office before I said something really dumb, like "I quit."

I couldn't leave—not now.

I'd been at the paper for over a year. My longest record for holding down a job had been my eighteen-month undistinguished tenure at Disney World, where I sold Epcot passes, sang "It's a Small World" until my throat ached, and swept up cigarette butts after the nightly fireworks display. If I could stand that kind of labor, I could stand anything. Besides, I had Kong, my teacup poodle, to consider. He couldn't take another move.

Bernice would not defeat me. If she wanted me to be a walking billboard, so be it. There were worse things in life: like being broke and unemployed.

Absolutely not an option.

With renewed determination, I drove toward Mango Bay,

my air conditioner turned off and my truck windows open, letting the hot air blow the panicked thoughts out of my brain like loose sand in a summer breeze. It didn't matter that Rusty was only a few degrees cooler than a sauna without the air conditioner chugging its meager puffs. I needed the calming whiff of humidity.

As I pulled into my spot at the Twin Palms RV Resort, I heaved a sigh of relief. My gleaming silver Airstream with its blue and white striped awning seemed invincible, all 4,225 pounds rooted in its familiar location under a palm tree and within sight of the small beach. Coral Island ran north/south, tucked inside a string of ritzy barrier islands, so it didn't boast the kind of beach that one normally expects in Florida. This was only a dollop of gray sand, with a few sea oats or shells, but I loved it just the same.

Most days it felt like nirvana.

All of a sudden, I remembered my sunburned face, and I touched my hands to my cheeks. They still felt warm. I could almost hear the popping of new freckles beneath my fingers.

I reached for the aloe bottle and ducked under the shade of my awning while I applied another layer. I slapped some on my raw feet, too, just to play it safe.

While doing so, I noticed an RV had parked in the space next to mine, although calling it an RV was like calling Rusty a Cadillac. It appeared more like a tattered tenement on wheels. Dirty yellow, with the snub-nosed front popular twenty years ago, it stood like a crumpled beacon of used-up aluminum.

Not that my Airstream was new by any stretch of the imagination, but I'd meticulously restored it and kept the silver hull buffed and shiny. My Airstream was historic; this RV was a hunk of junk.

Someone opened a window, and loud, sixties "geezer rock" emanated from within the yellow horror. *Oh, no.* Aging hippies. I'd had their kind parked next to me before at the Twin Palms, and it was a nightmare. All day and night they'd crank up old Bob Dylan and Rolling Stones songs, singing along with them, strolling around in love beads, tie-dyed T-shirts, and bell-bottoms. I shuddered to think what I was going to be subjected to over the next few days.

First thing in the morning, I'd talk to Wanda Sue, the owner of the Twin Palms RV Resort, about moving them. And I'd enlist the aid of Pop Pop Welch, the park's ancient, semi-mummified handyman, to keep an eye peeled for any infraction of the rules that might encourage them to move south toward the Keys.

"Could you keep the music down?" I called out.

Laughter emanated from the ramshackle RV, and the music volume spiked up a couple of notches. *Here we go with the Sixties Hit Parade.*

I wrenched open the door to my RV, and Kong leaped into my arms.

"How's my buddy?" I buried my face in his soft apricot fur while he licked my ear. Ah, the unconditional love of a teacup poodle. That was something—especially when the current men in my life either blew hot and cold (Nick) or traveled to and fro (Cole). *Don't think about that now.* I sighed and reached for Kong's leash, then fastened it to his collar. "Come on, let's hit the beach."

At the dreaded word *beach,* Kong tucked his head under my arm. Even after a year, he still recoiled from the water. I'd tried coaxing him with treats, playing soothing New Age music, even consulting the doggy psychologist in Orlando who'd suggested I name him King Kong in the first place to compensate for his inferiority complex caused by his diminutive size. She proposed that I deal with his "water issues" by showing him movies of beach scenes where people were having fun.

So for two months I'd rented corny movies like *Beach Blanket Bingo* and made him watch them. That still didn't help. And I got so sick of seeing Annette and Bobby in one smarmy love scene after another, I could've screamed.

So now we'd resorted to doing his business under an areca palm, followed by a brief stroll down to the surf. As I splashed in the waves to rinse my poor, dried-out feet, he kept a discreet distance, skittering away from even the tiniest drop of salt water.

After I filled him in on my day, we retreated to the Airstream, windows rammed shut, air-conditioning blasting in vain hopes of shutting out the aging hipsters' music.

I fed Kong his special gourmet organic doggy food and tossed a TV dinner into the microwave for me, too weary to do anything more ambitious. Actually, I never cooked even when I did have the energy. Fast and frozen food were my way of life.

The phone's melodious ring interrupted my activities. *Ah, music to my ears.* With my newfound financial stability, I'd traded up from my cheapie "deluxe" phone with a ring so shrill that Kong's fur would stand up, to a purring cordless with an answering machine.

Still, I picked up the receiver cautiously. This was usually the time my mother called with yet another update on my successful sister and equally successful brother. I wasn't in the mood. I'd found a body this morning and was staring into the possibility of having another murder on my hands. I needed to regroup, not regress.

"Hiya, kiddo," a familiar raspy voice greeted me.

"Anita? Is that you?"

"No, it's the First Lady," she chortled. "The White House is holding a reception for you."

My jaw clenched. "Where are you?"

"I'm on va-cay-tion." She enunciated each syllable with noticeable sarcasm. "Didn't Sandy tell you?"

"As a matter of fact, she did." I paused, holding on to my patience. I needed her to come back—soon. "And . . . so did your sister, Bernice."

"She's been in already? Good."

"What!" I exclaimed, letting my irritation out. "She doesn't have *any* journalism experience, she doesn't know the first thing about editing, and she's obsessed with bringing in these tacky advertisers." I took in a deep breath. "For Pete's sake, Bernice runs a charter fishing business. I don't think she's even *read* a newspaper. She probably uses them to wrap up fish for her customers like some crummy little fish-and-chips joint. I can't imagine what possessed you to have her step in while you're gone. Sandy and I are at our wit's end, and it's only the first day, and—"

Another cackle emanated from the other end of the phone. "I see Bernice hasn't found a way to stop your motormouth."

"This isn't funny, Anita. We've worked hard to maintain the integrity of our paper. It might be only an island weekly, but we publish good stories, and people respect what we do. A week of Bernice could seriously damage our reputation—"

"Don't get your feathers ruffled, kiddo. Bernice may have some good ideas. . . ."

"Like having Sandy and me wear T-shirts for anyone who buys advertising?" I gave an exclamation of disbelief. "How is that going to improve our paper?"

"That Bernice. She always did know how to make a buck."

"*Anita!* I don't think you're taking this seriously enough." I glanced at Kong for reassurance; he was licking a paw. I decided to take another tack with my MIA boss. "Is this something they'd do at the *Detroit Free Press*? What would your colleagues think of you if they knew what was going on at our paper?"

"Hah! Most of them have traded in their ideals for stock options and retirement plans."

Okay. That one wasn't going to work. Time to bring out the big guns. "I didn't want to tell you this and ruin your vacation or anything, but it looks as if we might have another murder on the island."

"What? Who?" Her voice grew more interested.

"Gina Fernandez, the Mango Queen." I filled her in on the details in a motormouth minute waltz.

"Sorry to hear that about Gina. She was a good kid who worked hard. Mama Maria must be cut to pieces."

"She is."

"All I can tell you is, keep your focus, kiddo. Follow the story, and press Nick Billie for details when you can."

"Bernice might make that difficult to—"

"You can handle her."

"But—"

"Kiddo, you're what we used to call a 'body magnet.' "

"What's that supposed to mean?"

"Whenever there's a body, you seem to be there. Don't worry—it's a good quality for a reporter. Some journalists go their whole lives without ever seeing so much as one corpse. You've seen three now, and it's only been your first year on Coral Island."

"Lucky me." What the heck was I doing wrong?

"I'll say. I've only seen half a dozen in thirty years."

Leave it to Anita to keep a head count. "Does Mr. Benton know you've put Bernice in charge?"

She laughed. "Yeah, he knows."

I detected another guffaw in the background. A masculine

one. All of a sudden something clicked in my brain. Benton was gone. Anita was gone. Had they gotten *that* chummy when the office was being repainted last year? *Double yuck.* "All right, Anita. Fess up. Is Mr. Benton with you?"

"She wants to know if you're here with me," Anita said, directing her voice away from the receiver.

The man laughed again, and she hung up after instructing me to "hang in there."

Ohmygod. Anita and Benton. Hadn't my world been rocked enough today? Now I had to deal with the mental image of my skinny, gum-cracking, sixtyish boss hanging out with Mr. Benton, a short, stout, balding cheapskate.

I replaced the receiver and slowly sank onto my kitchen chair.

The phone rang again, and I stared at it, not daring to pick up. After five rings, the answering machine kicked in, and I listened.

"Mallie? Are you there? It's Sam. I wanted to remind you to bring your sparring gear to Tae Kwon Do tonight and—"

I snatched up the receiver as if it were a lifeline and not just Sam, the island's metaphysical handyman and my Tae Kwon Do mentor. "I'm here. I was screening calls."

"Are you okay? You sound funny."

"It's been one of those days—the kind where you want to curl up under the covers and hide for the rest of the week."

"It's only Monday. You're not going to do that," he replied with thinly veiled amusement in his voice. "Come to class tonight. You need it. And you can tell me all about your day."

"You sure?"

"Yup. See you in an hour."

As I hung up, my mood lightened. Sam was one of the smartest people I knew—and the most patient. He'd help me make sense of today.

My glance fell to the tee from the Frozen Flamingo where I had flung it onto the table.

That might be too much, even for Sam.

An hour later, I strolled into the Island Health and Fitness Center, wearing the white pants from my Tae Kwon Do uniform, called a *dobok,* along with the Frozen Flamingo T-shirt.

A few muscle-bound guys doing free weights threw me wolf whistles. "It pays to advertise, babe," one of them joked.

"Thanks a lot."

I quickly moved into the small room off to the left where we had Tae Kwon Do class. Sam was already there, his black belt tied neatly around his trim waist. He was close to sixty but had that ageless look of a man totally at peace with himself. Head mostly bald, a tiny gold hoop in one ear, he appeared to be a cross between the guy-next-door and the Dalai Lama. Sam could talk about Descartes or the current *American Idol* and fix whatever ailed your house—or trailer, in my case—all in one visit.

The Jordan twins, Morgan and Megan, were already there warming up, along with a tall, broad-shouldered guy who had his back to me. I allowed the blue-belted twins one envious glance. At seventeen, they could kick as high as professional dancers and move like lightning. I hated sparring with either one of them because I always ended up with bruises from head to toe. They showed no mercy to someone of my advanced age of twenty-nine.

"Mallie, what'd ya do? Put your face in an oven?" Megan sniggered.

"No, I used the microwave."

"Morgan, Megan, finish your warm-up." Sam motioned them to the barre so they could stretch their legs. As if they needed it. Then he turned to me, concern in his eyes. "What happened?"

"At the last minute, I was given the assignment to cover the Little Coral Island trail opening this morning. I didn't realize it would take almost three hours to hike it. You know my skin and the sun."

"Did you get some aloe?"

"I bought some lotion right after the walk."

"No, you need to take the raw stalks from the plant, split them open, and rub the gel on your face. There are some growing outside—I'll break off a couple of pieces for you after class."

"Mucho thanks, my friend."

He eyed my Frozen Flamingo tee. "Nice shirt."

"That's only *part* of this day from hell." As we stretched together, I gave him an abbreviated version of the sequence of events from finding Gina's body to being transformed into a human billboard.

The only part that caused a reaction from him was my meeting with Aunt Lily. A mere flicker behind his eyes, but I caught it nonetheless. "So, what do you think? Was she right in asking me to investigate Gina's death? More important, will I end up telling off Bernice before the end of the week?"

"I think I need to mull it over. Let's finish our talk after class."

"But—"

"Exercise first. Then we'll solve the problems of Mallie's Mad World."

Reluctantly I nodded and slipped my jacket over my head. Then I wrapped my white belt with its yellow tip around my waist. It had taken me six months to earn the tip, which meant I was halfway to my yellow belt. God only knew how long it would take to actually have a colored belt, but I was determined to stick it out—if only to show those annoying Jordan twins.

"We've got a new member in class tonight," Sam announced as we lined up to bow in. "I think you all know him."

I glanced past the Jordan twins and beheld Nick Billie, looking all-powerful and sexy in a *dobok* and black belt.

"You do martial arts?" I sputtered.

"For ten years." He tightened his belt and straightened his jacket. "I've been working out in my garage for a while, but Sam convinced me I needed to be back in a formal class again."

"Oh." *Nice comeback.*

"Nick is going to be your sparring partner tonight," Sam pronounced as he took his position in front us.

My pulse jolted as a tiny thrill snaked through me. I'd be doing contact sports with Nick Billie tonight—the man who caused me to go weak in the knees. The man who sparked a physical attraction from me that could light up a Christmas tree. The man who had held my hand under the black mangrove tree only this morning. *Wow.*

And I thought I'd had an eventful day thus far.

The fireworks were only beginning.

Chapter Six

We moved through our usual class activities of punching and kicking drills, took a short water break, and then practiced our *kata*—the sequence of movements that simulate actual combat. Everyone else looked as if they were performing ballet moves. I, however, resembled an injured bird trying to take flight but never quite making it off the ground. It wasn't that I didn't try hard. I did. But my sense of balance consisted of being able to stand on one foot for maybe thirty seconds.

Nick Billie, of course, executed each move in the class with precision and grace. And I couldn't help but notice his rippling muscles under the *dobok* jacket. If anything, he looked even more powerful in his Tae Kwon Do uniform than he did in his usual jeans and button-down shirt. *Hot.*

"All right. I want you to pair up with a sparring partner," Sam said, as he pulled out the thick, padded mats. "First, we'll do some throws, then move into free sparring."

Oh, joy. My two *least* favorite parts of class.

Nick and I strode onto the mat and stood face-to-face.

"Which throws have you learned?" he asked.

"The first five."

"Go ahead and do them to me. Then I'll practice on you."

I eyed his wide shoulders. He looked tough, lean, and sinewy. How in the world would I ever be able to throw him anywhere?

Sam appeared at my side. "Remember, size isn't important in martial arts. Everyone can be brought down with the right kind of force exerted on pressure points."

I took in a deep breath and started my first throw. I grabbed Nick's jacket, pulled him toward me as I slipped my right foot behind his ankle. Then I swept his leg forward and twisted him backward onto the mat.

"Wow, I did it." My eyes widened in surprise at the sight of Nick Billie lying at my feet.

He swept his right foot around in an arc, catching me around the ankles. I thumped down onto the mat next to him, jarring everything inside me—including the potato chips I'd eaten on my way to the fitness center.

"Don't assume your opponent is immobilized just because he's down," Sam pointed out.

"That wasn't fair," I protested as I struggled to my feet and brushed off my bruised ego. "You said I was doing my throws first."

"Part of the throw is getting out of the way after your opponent is down." Nick grinned as he rose in one fluid movement.

"Thanks for the warning. I'll make sure I do that next time." I proceeded to do my next four throws, trying to slam him onto the mat with all the force I could—and stepping back when the move was over. Needless to say, he didn't drop nearly hard enough. Somehow he barely made contact with the mat and would roll back onto his feet. He was like a jungle cat. Wouldn't you just know?

"I'm going to show you some new moves." Nick grasped

my belt and pulled me close. His face moved to within inches of mine. We locked glances, his dark eyes fastened on me with that smoldering intensity that I found mesmerizing.

"What . . . what are you going to do to me?" My mouth turned as dry as cotton candy.

"Just this." He raised one knee and twisted me around it. As he dropped his leg, I fell to the mat—yet again.

"Cool move," Megan enthused. "Could you do it to her again, so I can learn it?"

"Me too," Morgan piped up.

I glared at both of them as I struggled to my feet. "I'm not a human guinea pig."

"Let Nick demonstrate a couple of times," Sam said. "It's all part of learning."

"Easy for you to say," I muttered under my breath.

"Hey, I was careful not to let you drop too hard." Nick grasped my belt again. "Trust me, I won't hurt you."

He repeated the move, though he kept a hold on my belt, so I didn't break a leg or anything. My pride was the only thing bruised—as usual. Megan and Morgan clapped every time I hit the mat, and I began to plot different ways to take my revenge on the twins from hell. Images of "accidentally" tossing gum into their hair floated through my mind. Or spilling a whole bottle of Gatorade into their gym bags "by mistake."

Finally, the throw humiliation ended, and we took a water break. Drenched in sweat, I knew my sunburned face must've been the color of a cooked beet.

"You looked good out there," Nick said, lounging against a wall, water bottle in hand.

"Good? I was squashed on the mat like a mosquito under your hand." I gulped down my Gatorade.

"It's all part of martial arts training. You have to know who's in charge." One side of his mouth crooked upward.

"Oh, pleeeeease." I bristled. "You might be a higher belt in the *dojang,* but that doesn't mean you're superior to me in any other way."

"But I might know things that you don't. And not just in the martial arts. I've been on this island a lot longer than you have." He took a swig of water, and his expression turned almost playful. What? Nick Billie acting mischievous?

"I've learned a lot in the year I've lived here." My eyes narrowed. "Wait a minute. Are you talking about Gina Fernandez?"

"I might be."

"Did you find out anything about her death?"

"Maybe." He took another casual drink of water. "I heard you were asking a lot of questions again—at Mama Maria's, at Island Décor—"

"Only for background information on my article about Gina's death." That was sort of true.

"Be careful." His voice turned a bit more serious. "Her death is going to affect a lot of people on Coral Island, and no one is going to take too kindly to an . . . outsider digging up dirt on the Mango Queen."

Outsider! It was on the tip of my tongue to start arguing with him, but I was in the *dojang.* I had to behave with courtesy. Besides, I'd learned that butting heads with Nick Billie— even if he were more relaxed than usual—did nothing except give me a headache. "So, Gina was well liked?" I tilted my head upward with a polite expression of inquiry.

"By most."

"She was certainly attractive. I'll bet she made a striking Mango Queen. I'm just sorry I didn't do a story on her getting the crown a couple of nights ago."

His eyes turned somber. "At least Gina had that. I don't think I've ever seen a person look happier."

"Wasn't she a shoo-in to win? I gathered from what Brandi

said this morning that Gina had been campaigning all year to become Mango Queen."

"All island women wanted the title, but Gina and Brandi coveted it the most. From what I heard, they were neck and neck right up till the final judging."

"So it was down to the two of them?"

Nick finished his water and threw the empty bottle into his gym bag. "One judge's decision threw the vote Gina's way. It was four/three split."

"That must've been quite a blow to Brandi." I replaced the cap on my Gatorade. "Of course, now that Gina is gone, she'll be the Mango Queen."

"What are you getting at?"

I shrugged. "Nothing. Just making an observation. You don't happen to know the name of the judge who cast the deciding ballot, do—"

"All right, Mallie, you can cut the nicey-nice routine. I like you better when you're spitting at me like a wildcat. At least I know where you're coming from."

"And I prefer you when you're rigid and unyielding. Then I know where *you're* coming from." I gave him a wink. "All I did was ask an innocent question."

He burst out with a throaty laugh. "There's no such thing as an 'innocent' question from you—especially when it involves a suspicious death."

"So you *do* think there could've been foul play."

"I didn't say that."

"But you hinted—"

"Look, I told you I'd let you know when I had the autopsy results. Until then, it's idle speculation to think that Gina's death was caused by anything other than natural causes."

I raised my eyebrows. "What about the syringe that was next to her body? I'd hardly call that 'natural'—"

"Shh." He placed an index finger over his mouth. "I don't want the whole *dojang* to hear—especially those two blabbermouth twins. If they get wind of anything, it'll be all around the island by lunchtime tomorrow."

I glanced across the room and noticed that the usually boisterous duo had become very quiet and had started to drift in our direction.

"Just because that syringe was there doesn't mean Gina used it," he pointed out in a low voice. "It could've been left in the grass by someone else days ago."

I turned back to him. "But what if her prints are on it?"

He paused. "Then we'll be a step closer to knowing what happened."

I touched his arm. "It's not only for the newspaper. I want to know what happened to Gina. She had everything going for her, and to have her life end so suddenly . . . It's just tragic."

His hand covered mine. "I feel the same way."

Sparks shot up my arm from his fingers.

"Okay, break time is over." Sam slapped Nick on the back. "We've got a few more self-defense techniques to work on."

Nick dropped his hand and moved away.

"You two looked mighty cozy," Sam commented.

"Let's just say we finally agreed on something." I tightened my belt.

"Such as?"

"I'll fill you in after class."

He led me to the center of the *dojang,* where we worked on a few self-defense moves, none of which I could do very well. Then we did some push-ups and, finally, ended class. Needless to say, I was drenched in sweat once again, whereas Nick barely had a few beads of perspiration on his forehead.

The twins left, whispering and pointing in my direction on their way out. I glared in response, which elicited giggles.

"It feels good to be back in class," Nick said to Sam as he loosened his black belt and removed his *dobok* jacket.

My mouth almost dropped open as his bare chest was revealed: a magnificent, finely muscled upper torso. In fact, it was one of the sexiest I'd ever seen, not that I'd seen all that many recently—just those of the elderly retirees who walked the beach at the Twin Palms. And those sagging pecs weren't a pleasant sight, let me tell you.

Breathless, I dabbed at my face with a towel, hoping they'd think it was because of the push-ups and not because the sight of Nick Billie's bare chest had gotten me all hot and bothered.

Nick reached into his gym bag and pulled out a white T-shirt. As he slipped it over his head, I took one last look at the black curly hair that covered his chest. *Yummy.*

"Wait here, Mallie. I want to get some aloe stalks for your sunburn." After Sam exited, we stood there in awkward silence. Was it possible Nick could tell that a wave of attraction had just rolled over me with the power of a tropical storm?

I cleared my throat. "So, you're going to call me with that autopsy report in a day or two?"

"Don't you think about anything else?"

"Not when my job is on the line."

"I thought you liked moving around."

For a moment, the lure of the open road appeared in my mind, and I could see myself in my truck, driving my Airstream and teacup poodle to our next adventure. I cut off the fantasies. That was the old Mallie. "This is where I belong—for now. And now that I've got Bernice the Butthead forcing me to do her version of 'reality journalism,' I've got to watch my back and keep my focus. I need that information as soon as you get it."

He chuckled and tweaked my chin. "Sure." He heaved his gym bag over his shoulder. "I'll call you." On his way out, he murmured a couple of words to Sam, who was coming back in, stalks of aloe in hand. I couldn't make out what he said, but Sam looked at me with an odd expression. What in the world had gotten into Nick Billie? Had the island cop gone soft?

"What were you two talking about?" I asked, watching as Sam slit open the aloe stalk's thick green skin.

"Just man talk."

"Thanks a lot. Now you evoke the macho brotherhood on me."

"Hardly that." He scooped out a glob of clear, sticky liquid. "Nick and I go way back. I've known him since he first came to the island."

"What was he like then?"

"Pretty much the same." He rubbed the gooey stuff all over my face.

"Yuck." I inhaled with a grimace. "It smells like an old tire."

"Aloe has healing properties—trust me. By tomorrow, the redness will be way down."

"What about the freckles?"

He smiled down at me. "I think those are terminal."

We both laughed.

"Seriously, what makes Nick Billie tick?" I slipped off my *dobok* jacket. "I know all about that case on the Miccosukee Reservation when he was with the tribal police and a young boy died. That's why he came here to Coral Island. I'd like to know more about him . . . personally."

Sam said nothing for a few minutes as he brushed the excess aloe gel off my face. "He's a complicated man. Getting close to him might be more than you're ready for. You could get tangled in the thorns."

"What do you mean? He's been sort of . . . nice recently."

"Roses have thorns. They are sensual, attractive, but you never know when you might get hurt."

"Oh, come on." I waved a dismissive hand. "He can't be that dangerous."

Sam leveled a long, low glance in my direction. "I think we both know he is."

Something stirred uneasily inside of me. "Maybe you're right. I'm not sure I'm ready for that kind of involvement. My old boyfriend, Cole, is coming to visit, and he's . . ." My voice trailed off.

"Safer?" Sam split another aloe stalk and handed it to me.

"More predictable. More like the guys I've always dated. I don't think love has to be this heavy, gut-wrenching experience. It should be light and happy and carefree."

"That's not love, Mallie—that's just hanging out together. Real love turns your soul inside out."

I held up a hand. "If that's love, I don't want it."

"Then you'd better stay away from Nick. Because he's just the kind of man to shake you to the core."

"This discussion is all academic." I tossed my jacket into my gym bag, holding my nose while I unzipped. I'd bought the bag in my favorite used-clothing store on the island, Secondhand Rose, and in spite of many, many washings, it still smelled like a pile-driver's lunchbox on a sweltering day. "Nick's not really boyfriend material anyway."

"Don't be too sure. I've never seen him get so hot and bothered over a woman." He grinned.

The implication sent waves of excitement through me. But they were quickly followed by tides of caution. Sparring verbally or physically with Nick was one thing, but anything deeper scared the hell out of me.

I heaved the gym bag over my shoulder. "Maybe it's best Nick and I keep things on a professional level. I'm a reporter, after all. Getting to know Nick on a personal level could be a . . . a conflict of interest."

"Coward."

"That's my middle name. Mallie C. Monroe."

"I wouldn't say that." His eyes seemed to twinkle. "You might want more than a man like Cole can offer you. You've changed since you came to Coral Island."

My mind raced back to scenes of seeing my first dead body last summer, rescuing a young boy, comforting a woman who'd lost her husband, facing down not one, but two murderers—and finding another dead body this morning.

"Yeah, my first year working at the *Observer* has been eventful, to say the least."

"Nick Billie might be your next trial by fire."

"I think I'd rather walk over live coals," I murmured as I strolled past him.

He followed, then closed the door and locked it behind him. "You won't have to do the 'fire walk' until you test for your black belt."

"What?" I stopped in my tracks.

"Just kidding."

"Whew." I brushed my fingers across my forehead.

"No—worse. You'll have to break a concrete block."

"That's a piece of cake compared to getting caught in Nick Billie's 'thorns.' " I climbed into Rusty and rolled the window down. About three-quarters of the way, it stuck, and the handle jammed. Typical. Rusty got temperamental after dark. Pulling on the neck of my Frozen Flamingo tee, I fanned myself.

Sam remained stationed outside my window. "Be careful asking around about Gina Fernandez. Her fiancé's family has a lot of money and power," he warned. "Everyone knew they didn't like the idea of her becoming their daughter-in-law. Brett was being groomed for a political career, and having a wife who was the granddaughter of a migrant worker wouldn't have helped."

"That's sort of what Aunt Lily said."

"Lily's spent a lifetime on this island and knows everybody's secrets—and then some. I'd trust her instincts about everything. Life, death, and . . . love."

I peered at him closely. Did Sam's attachment to Aunt Lily go beyond friendship? Her husband, Uncle Rich, had died in World War II, and she'd been a grieving widow ever since. At least that was the story passed around my family. Was there more to it than that?

"Sam, are you suggesting that Aunt Lily is—"

"I'm not saying anything other than she's a very wise, compassionate woman." Sam's face shuttered into silence.

But there was more. I could feel the unspoken words between us.

He tapped my door twice and stepped back. "If the Palmers had something to do with Gina's death, they'll be protected by their wealth. And they won't hesitate to get rid of anyone who might bring them down. Be careful." He gave a little wave and disappeared into the night.

I understood. If I found incriminating evidence linking the Palmers to Gina's death, they'd come after *me.*

I fanned myself a second time, but not because of the heat.

Chapter Seven

By the time I left Tae Kwon Do class, the day's events began to catch up with me. My whole body sagged with fatigue behind the wheel, and my face burned from the sun-lashing it had received that morning.

My Airstream beckoned. Home.

As I headed back to the Twin Palms RV Resort, unpleasant images of the day flitted through my mind like a flashback in a movie: Gina's body under the black mangrove tree, Aunt Lily's tearful face, Mama Maria smashing crystal with gut-wrenching grief, Rivas' anger, and then . . . Nick Billie shirtless after Tae Kwon Do.

Oops . . . not so negative.

At least *that* image caused a shot of high-octane energy to course through me. Not to mention some tingling in my still-salty toes.

But it lasted only briefly, and another wave of fatigue descended over me like a heavy blanket.

I pressed down the pedal to get to Rusty's maximum speed of 55 mph. *Come on, baby, get me back to my Airstream.* The sooner I got back to Mango Bay, the sooner I could drop into bed and forget about everything that had happened to me today—the good and the bad.

Within ten minutes, I pulled into the spot next to my trailer, anticipating the quiet of the RV park. I slid out of Rusty and stumbled toward my Airstream. Then it hit me: a blast of the Rolling Stones' song "(I Can't Get No) Satisfaction." *Jeez.* I pivoted on my heel and advanced toward the ramshackle RV next door, my eyes narrowed, ready for a battle.

I banged on the corroded aluminum siding of the tenement on wheels and shouted: "Quiet time is after ten o'clock! Turn down the music, or I'll call Wanda Sue!"

Laughter emanated from within, but the volume lowered a few notches.

"Idiots," I muttered under my breath as I made for my Airstream. I vowed to talk to Wanda Sue, owner/manager of the Twin Palms, tomorrow about expelling them from the site. She took any violations of the park's rules very seriously indeed. And if those infractions were reported by the few of us who lived here year-round, the perpetrators would be toast.

I opened the door and was greeted by the loving paws of Kong. He must've sensed my ready-to-drop tiredness because he took only a brief walk to do his business, and in no time flat, we were stretched out in bed, side by side, drifting off to sleep. My last conscious thought was of Gina. . . . It seemed so unfair for her life to end just at the point when she had everything: a wealthy fiancé, a good job, and the Mango Queen title.

Poor Gina. . . .

The soft ring of my phone awakened me early the next morning. I groaned, ducked under the pillow, and curled it around my ears. *Oh, no.* I couldn't take my mother this morning. Or, worse, Anita.

But the phone wouldn't stop—and I'd turned off my answering machine last night. *Damn.*

I reached out and picked up the receiver, slipping it under the pillow toward my ear. "Hello?"

No answer.

"Hel-LO?"

I heard breathing on the other end, but no one spoke.

"Look, if this is an obscene phone call, forget it. I heard every kind of nasty language going when I was a ticket-taker for short-tempered parents at Disney World."

More breathing.

I gave an exasperated sigh and slammed the receiver down. Lifting one end of the pillow, I checked my alarm clock. Six-thirty A.M. *No way.* I pounded the mattress and tried to will myself back to sleep. I counted sheep. I counted palm trees. I counted mangos.

Nothing worked.

Wide awake, I threw back the covers and sat up, stroking Kong. Who the hell would call me so early? My number was unlisted, but that didn't mean much these days. People had a hundred illicit ways to find out your phone number. I shrugged. Probably just a wrong number.

Still, a sense of caution tugged at the back of my mind. Whoever had called me had hung on the line, breathing and saying nothing—just so I'd know someone was there.

"Whaddya think, Kong? What kind of creep would get up this early just to do some heavy breathing?"

His brown button eyes gazed up at me with no answer, but the rapid wag of his tail told me it was time for a walk. I hooked the leash onto his collar, threw on a T-shirt and shorts, and cautiously stepped out of my Airstream, gazing out over the horizon.

Mercifully, it was quiet.

The sun rose, a golden ball in a sapphire-tinted sky, casting shimmering lights on the Gulf of Mexico. I turned my face toward the light, and, gradually, warm waves radiated down, with only a slight breeze coming in off the Gulf. *A new dawn, a new day.*

Kong and I strolled toward the beach, with my tugging him as we drew near the surf.

"Hey, Mallie, you're up early," Wanda Sue said as she approached, carrying a large green plastic bag and one of those sticks with a prong at the end to spear trash without bending over.

In spite of the early hour, she sported her usual carefully coiffed beehive and flamboyant attire: sleeveless, tropical-print top and pink spandex shorts. *Classy.*

As I approached, she poked at a Styrofoam cup and tossed it into the trash bag.

"Don't you hate it when people treat the beach like their own person garbage can? I swear, it makes me hopping mad as a jackrabbit. I'm gonna put out a notice to everyone in the park that if they get caught littering, they're outta here faster than you can say 'Who shot Jimmy?' "

"Who's Jimmy?"

Wanda Sue laughed. "It's just an expression, honey. Sometimes I forget you're not from around here."

"So it's a generic Jimmy?"

"Huh?" Her overplucked eyebrows arched upward.

"Never mind." I picked up a dented soda can and handed it to her. "I'm glad I ran into you. Those yahoos in the site next to me were blasting rock music last night after quiet time."

She sighed and tossed the can into the trash bag. "You're not the first person to complain. I asked Pop Pop to talk to them today."

Oh, boy. Pop Pop Welch lived on the property in a five-hundred-square-foot cottage that looked as if a strong puff of wind could blow it away. Since Pop Pop was on the high side of seventy, that pretty much described his frail physical state too. He was supposed to be in charge of security, among his other duties, but he usually took out his hearing aids at night, so I didn't put a lot of faith in his ability to take on nighttime marauders, much less my noisy neighbors.

"Maybe *you* need to lay down the law to them, Wanda Sue." I reeled out Kong's leash, and he scampered away from the water. "I had to beat on the side of their trailer last night and threaten to call you to get any kind of response."

She stiffened. "Did they come out?"

"No. Just laughed their fool heads off. But they did turn down the volume."

Visibly, she relaxed again. "Don't you worry none, honey. I'll take care of the situation. They're not gonna be here all that long—maybe only a few days."

My eyes narrowed. "Is there something you're not telling me?"

"No, of course not. I'd never hide anything important from you." She blinked her spiky, mascara-laden lashes but didn't quite meet my gaze. "Not after all you've done for me, what with saving my grandson's life."

"All I did was help Detective Billie find him." My thoughts harked back to last fall, when I had accompanied Nick on a rescue mission to find Wanda Sue's grandson. We found him all right—along with his father's dead body. I shuddered inwardly and tried to clear those thoughts from my mind. "What are friends for?"

"Well, I'll never forget it. You're in my BFF book, Mallie Monroe. And you know what that means."

I smiled weakly. "Discount coupons at the island Subway?"

"You betcha." She patted me on the shoulder. "I've got a drawer full of coups for a free six-inch sub."

"Thanks." An old motor-court building at the island center had recently been renovated into a Subway. In no time flat, it had become the island hub. Personally, I liked my fast food greasy and full of fat, so I rarely frequented its hallowed portals. "Did you hear about Gina Fernandez?"

"Sure did." Wanda Sue's face turned grim. "I got the news this morning at the Island Hardware from Old Man Brisbee. It made me sadder than get-out, honey. My goodness . . . our Mango Queen. She was a lovely gal too. Poor Mama Maria must be plumb out of her mind with grief. I'll have to go over to her restaurant later and pay my respects."

"I'm sure she'd appreciate that," I said as Kong finally ran out of leash and began to trot back. "I guess you also heard that I found the . . . uh . . . body."

"Yeah, that's gone around the island like a brush fire." Her mouth pursed. "But I don't for one single minute believe what some people are saying about you—"

"What's that?"

She hesitated.

"Come on, Wanda Sue, give it to me. I'm a big girl. I can take it."

"Some people—and I'm not giving any names, mind you— think you're a bad omen."

I rolled my eyes. "Just because I was the one who saw Gina's body first?"

"Mallie." She leveled a long, serious glance in my direction. "This is the third time you've found a dead person on Coral Island. . . ."

"Wait a minute. The second time, when it was Kevin's dad, Nick Billie was with me. So, technically, that one doesn't count."

"I'm afraid that's not how people see it."

"What do you mean?" I spread my hands in helpless appeal. "Everyone is going to avoid me like the proverbial plague now?"

"Can't say, honey. You're gonna need to talk to an expert on this kind of thing. Someone who's got a lot more experience than me."

"Who? An exorcist?" I couldn't resist the sarcasm creeping into my voice. I'd tried hard to be part of the quirky Coral Island community, and, for the first time in my life, I had a place where I seemed to belong. A stable job—sort of. A permanent home—kind of. A circle of friends—maybe.

"An exhibitionist? Don't be silly, honey. Not that we don't have some of them people on the island. You know, there was talk of a nudist colony here, but . . . oh, I'm getting off the subject." She tapped her forehead, presumably to knock her thoughts back on track. "You need to see Madame Geri. She'll know what to do."

I groaned inwardly. Madame Geri was the island's freelance psychic who wrote a weekly astrology column for the *Observer* and, in my opinion, was one of the great all-time con artists. Not that she didn't come forth with a semi-accurate prediction now and again, but who couldn't with comments like, "You'll have a conflict this week" or "Be careful when driving." Heck, even *I* could "predict" *that.*

Last year, Anita had insisted I allow Madame Geri to tag along during the murder investigation of Kevin Crawford's father. I'd put up with her constant craziness and her beady-eyed bird companion, Marley, for almost a week. Granted, she did distract the murderer trying to stab me with a paint knife, but that barely made up for those interminable days of her New Age nuttiness.

Unfortunately, everyone on the island thought she was a sage somewhere between an Old Testament prophet and a modern-day shaman—or sha-woman, in this case.

"What can Madame Geri do?"

"She'll cleanse your aura."

"Huh?"

"Trust me, it won't hurt one bit. I've had it done myself lots of times—especially when I was feeling blue after my husband died. I just couldn't imagine running the Twin Palms without him. It was a dark time, let me tell you, honey. So I went to Madame Geri. She contacted her guide in the spirit world, and he told me that my dead hubby was just fine and dandy up there in heaven. That made me feel loads better. Then she cleansed my aura by running hot stones up and down my body till all the negative energy was gone. Ahhhhh, just talking about it makes me want to get a refresher. It might help the arthritis in my back."

During this long diatribe, my mouth had dropped open. "You aren't serious about this aura thing."

"Don't knock it till you've tried it."

"Thanks, but I think I'll pass. Anyway, I've got to get my butt to work. Bernice is running things now, and she might dock my pay if I'm late. See ya." I pulled in Kong's leash, and we hot-footed out of there before Wanda Sue could come up with any more lame suggestions for improving my personal life.

I showered, dressed in my jeans and the *Feast with Me at the Frozen Flamingo* tee, kissed Kong, and took off for the *Observer*. Of course, I made a quick stop for my usual extra-glazed Krispy Kreme doughnuts and coffee, downing them in my truck so as not to tempt Sandy to fall off the diet wagon any further.

As I entered the *Observer* office, yet again a strange odor assailed my senses. I sniffed. It wasn't bait this time. I sniffed again. It seemed more . . . earthy. I glanced at Sandy, who was downing the last bite of a gooey pastry. Her fiancé, Jimmy, perched near her, holding her hand. She wore a new T-shirt with the riveting image of a sawed-down palm tree and the logo *Steve's Stupendous Stump Removal.*

My eyes traveled over to the side of her desk. I gasped, one hand moving to cover my nose. The source of today's pungent smell revealed itself: a large stump, complete with dirt-encrusted roots. It sat on the floor atop old copies of the newspaper.

"Bernice's latest advertiser dropped it off early this morning." Sandy closed her eyes and leaned her head against Jimmy's shoulder.

"Steve Kimmel, the 'stump man'?" I stepped around the offensive object.

She raised her head. "You know him?"

I nodded. "He took out a couple of dead hibiscus bushes for Wanda Sue after the cold spell last fall. He . . . uh . . . seemed nice enough." What else could I say? We were working in an office with a stump.

"I don't know how much longer I can take this," Sandy moaned. "Sure, it doesn't even begin to compare with Gina's death yesterday, but I'm freaking out."

"No, you're not, sweetheart." Jimmy squeezed her hand. A fresh-faced young man with a broad, beefy physique, he was also unfailingly chipper. It was hard to believe that he couldn't help Sandy deal with anything that Bernice could dish out. It was even harder to believe that he was Madame Geri's son. How that phony psychic could have produced such a nice, normal boy was beyond me.

"Remember, Bernice's running the newspaper is only temporary. Once Anita returns, things will get back to normal." *Relatively speaking,* I added to myself. Who would've thought I'd be looking forward to seeing Anita? The woman who called me "kiddo" and smacked gum in my face. "Speaking of the devil—I mean, Anita—I talked with her yesterday."

Sandy perked up, her eyes kindling with hope. "Where is she? Is she coming back soon?"

"Well, there's good and bad news. The good: Anita is on vacation with . . . Mr. Benton."

"Anita and Mr. Benton? Barf city." Sandy motioned toward her open mouth with a finger in a mock gagging motion.

"My sentiments exactly. I guess they must have become . . . friendly last year when she finally persuaded him to hire Jimmy to paint the office. Or maybe it was a long-standing affair. Who knows?" With great effort, I blocked the image of Anita and Mr. Benton out of my mind. "More good news: I didn't get the impression they'd be gone too long."

"But what about Bernice?"

"That's the bad news." I sighed. "Anita put her in charge, all right. And Benton must've gone along with it. I tried to tell Anita what was going on, but she didn't want to hear it. She said, among other things, that we had to 'hang in there.' "

"So we're on our own with the boss from hell." Sandy's eyes dulled once more with despair.

"Looks like it," I replied.

"Hey, I'll get my mom over here," Jimmy piped up. "She'll know what to do."

"Does she have any voodoo dolls?" I asked, imagining a tiny version of Butthead Bernice that I could attack with a pin. Nothing fatal. Only enough pinpricks to incapacitate her until Anita grew tired of her middle-aged tryst with Mr. Benton.

Jimmy stood up, a slight expression of indignation on his open features. "As if Mom would resort to black magic. You know her better than that. She'll do a tarot reading or ask the spirit world for guidance. And she'll find some answers—trust me."

"Really?" Sandy clutched his hand.

"Sure." He smiled down at her with adoring eyes.

I refrained from groaning. Adding Madame Geri to the mix was like pouring gasoline onto a fire. "I'm not sure—"

"About what?" Bernice strode out of her cubicle, another lollipop in her mouth. Her attire still had the nautical theme, with an electric-blue striped top, but it was paired with very tight black leggings, revealing sags and bulges in places where I didn't want to go.

"About . . . uh . . . some of my interviews for the 'Terror on the Trail' article." I shot Jimmy a warning look.

"If you'd get in here at a reasonable hour, you might get some work done. We're not running a bank here, Miss Priss." She patted the stump. "You need to finish the trail story *and* Gina's obituary. I'm going to run them side by side. That'll really spike up the emotion a notch."

"But obituaries run on their own page . . . separate from the other stories. We don't want to seem to be exploiting Gina's death just to sell papers." I watched her pat the stump with a smile of approval.

"Of course we are. That's the point." She strolled forward. "We're doing reality journalism, and that means every dark area of life has to be exposed. The naked truth. That's what I want. Hell, it doesn't even have to be true, as long as it's sleazy."

I clenched my teeth. "I'll finish up the trail story this morning. Then I'll talk to Gina's fiancé and her mother for the obituary. But it's going to be respectful. After all, she was the Mango Queen. People on Coral Island aren't going to want to see her name dragged through the mud."

"You've got a lot to learn about human nature, Miss Priss," she informed me in an irritating, know-it-all tone. "The higher they are, the more readers delight in seeing them taken down a notch. Why do you think they sell so many tabloids about actors in rehab or actresses getting caught shoplifting? Get real.

There's nothing that sells papers like seeing how far the mighty can fall."

"Maybe so, but this is a hometown island girl, not some Hollywood bimbette. Gina grew up on Coral Island, and people loved her."

"Are you refusing to follow my orders?" Bernice slowly removed the lollipop from her mouth.

"I am." I stood firm, not flinching as her wrinkled, leathery face inched closer to mine.

The office became very quiet. I heard my heart thumping in my chest like a series of sonic booms. But I wasn't going to give in. Bernice could fire me. I knew it, and she knew it. But I would not let her turn Gina's death into some tawdry event— not after seeing the grief of Mama Maria and Rivas. They deserved to have Gina's memory honored.

All of a sudden, she stepped back. "Okay. I'll give you the tasteful obit for next week's edition of the *Observer.* But after that, I want a full investigative story for the next edition." She scowled at me. "No holds barred."

"Agreed." I managed to swallow the lump in my throat.

"Fine." She threw a T-shirt at me and marched back toward her cubicle. "Wear it."

I caught the shirt, not even needing to look at it. So I had to promote *Steve's Stupendous Stump Removal.* Who cared? I'd finally won a battle with Bernice the Butthead. *Yahoo!*

Bernice slammed the door.

Chapter Eight

Sandy clapped her hands silently, joy lighting her face. "Mallie, you're a marvel. How did you find the courage to stand up to that old bag?"

"I don't know what got into me." I pulled out my rickety wooden chair and collapsed into it.

"Sheer chutzpah," Sandy breathed.

"Spirit energy," Jimmy added.

"Shameless stupidity." I took in a couple of deep breaths.

"No, you were heroic." Sandy reached into her desk drawer and pulled out a package of cookies, half a dozen minicakes, and a bag of peanut M&M's. "And I can be too." She dumped all the sweets into the trash can.

"Sweetie, I'm so proud of you." Jimmy planted a kiss on her cheek.

"Me too." I smiled, pleased with both Sandy and myself. "We might be on our own here, but this is our turf. Bernice is the interloper. What we need to do is get proactive and beat her at her own game."

"You're right." Sandy mulled this over for a few minutes.

"Bernice wants new advertisers. But the only ones she seems to rope in are people she knows from hanging out at the Seafood Shanty—bait dealers, stump removers, and so on. What I need to do is find some people who want to advertise with us who run more . . . uh . . . upscale businesses. Attorneys, accountants—that kind of person. Chances are, they wouldn't want us to wear T-shirts or deposit a stump in the middle of the office."

"Yes!" I gave her a thumbs-up. "Brilliant. Call Aunt Lily. I'm sure she knows some people on the island who don't chew tobacco or eat with their fingers who'll want to advertise with us."

"Gotcha." Sandy picked up the phone.

"Mallie, that reminds me, I've got a message from Mom." Jimmy scooted his chair toward my desk.

"Oh?" Not a Madame Geri pseudo-prophecy. They had caused me nothing but trouble in the past.

"She said that since Gina died, the mango balance is off." He spoke with solemn gravitas.

"Okay." I motioned him with my fingers. "Give it to me: What's the 'mango balance'?"

"The whole aura that surrounds the island and makes it possible to grow the mangos. You know, our island is world-renowned for its varieties and quality. There are very few places that produce the kinds of mangos we have here. But it's a delicate balance between man and nature." He paused and leaned forward. "Gina was the Mango Queen, and now she's dead, so the balance has been disturbed."

"Let me get this straight: I not only need to get my aura cleansed—as per Wanda Sue's instructions—the whole island does too?" I gave a laugh of disbelief. "Brandi was the runner-up. I'm sure she'll take on the duties before the Mango Festival next weekend. Then the balance will be restored."

"That's what I said to Mom, but she told me the spirit world is disturbed. Something is off-kilter."

"Regarding Gina's death?"

"I don't know. She wants you to call her."

I rubbed my forehead with a weary hand. Stumps. Bernice the Butthead. Mango balance. Madame Geri. And it wasn't even lunchtime yet. "I don't know, Jimmy. When your mother gets involved, things have a way—"

"She knew you'd say that." He nodded with a smile. "She told me to tell you that if you want to know what happened to Gina, you need to phone her ASAP."

I frowned. That crazy clairvoyant had a knack for knowing what I wanted almost before I did. Not that it made her a psychic. She was just . . . perceptive.

"Do it, Mallie." Sandy covered the phone receiver with her hand. "It helped me to keep on the Ozone Diet. Just wanting to lose weight wasn't enough. I had to get rid of all that negative energy that kept me diving headfirst into high-caloric foods and—"

"You lost weight because of pure willpower," I corrected her.

"Uh-uh. It was the aura-cleansing. Trust me. In fact, after we get Bernice outta here, I'm going in for another cleansing." She patted her stomach. "I've got to clean out my M&M cravings."

"Waving good-bye to Bernice's backside should do it." I cleared my throat in a pointed effort to change the subject.

"Ooops . . ." Sandy removed her hand and spoke briefly into the receiver.

"Did Aunt Lily give you any names of potential advertisers?" I asked.

"She wasn't in. I left a message on her answering machine."

"Good. She knows everybody on the island. There's got to

be some better potential advertisers than Steve the Stump Remover."

"About that aura cleansing . . ." Jimmy began.

"I've really got to work on my 'Terror on the Trail' story." I swiveled away from him and flipped on the ancient Dell computer that Sandy and I shared. Unfortunately, the shaky chair legs creaked from the sudden movement, and one of the wheels flew off, causing one side to thump down to the floor.

Jimmy caught the rolling wheel under his foot, picked it up, and handed it to me. "See? This is what happens when your aura is cloudy."

"No." I snatched the wheel from him. "This is what happens when your employer is too cheap to buy decent office furniture."

I turned my attention to the computer.

Auras be damned.

After a couple of hours, I sat back, careful not to make too sudden of a move in my rickety chair. "Not bad," I murmured aloud as I scanned the story. No one answered. Sandy and Jimmy had left for a low-cal lunch at Subway, and Bernice had exited several hours ago, presumably to knock back a few beers at the Shanty. Hooray. At least the office was quiet for a little while.

The phone rang, and I picked up. "Hello?"

No response.

"Hel-LO!"

Heavy breathing greeted me at the other end.

"If you're the same person who called me at home, I'm not impressed." I slammed the received down.

Turning back to the computer, I noticed a tremor in my hands. Okay, this heavy breather was beginning to spook me a bit. How did the caller know I'd be the one to pick up the phone at work? Was someone watching me?

Slowly I peered over my shoulder toward the front window. Only dirty, dingy glass stared back at me. I laughed in nervous relief. *Get a grip. Nothing's going to happen at the* Observer *office. Too many people around.* A deli was located on one side and a florist on the other. Someone would notice if a marauder came into the office.

I took in a couple of deep breaths and said my Tae Kwan Do mantra: "Mugatoni." Most people chose something Zen-like; I chose something ziti-like. It instantly calmed me—and made me hanker for a plateful of pasta.

The phone rang again. Chewing on my lower lip, I stared at it this time. I wouldn't have to hear the breathing if I didn't pick up. But then again, it could be important news. This was a newspaper, after all.

With a hesitant hand, I picked up the receiver but said nothing.

"Mallie? It's Madame Geri."

"Oh, it's you," I gushed. "Thank goodness."

"No need to thank *me.* Marley was the one who told me not to wait but to call you today."

"He has my gratitude." I heard Madame Geri murmuring words of praise to the turquoise-feathered, beady-eyed bird who was her constant companion. He squawked, and I rolled my eyes. "Madame Geri? Are you calling to file next week's horoscopes or to talk about the 'aura cleansing'?"

"I already gave the astrology readings to Sandy yesterday, and I'm telling you, they weren't good. Mercury is in retrograde for the next ten days, which means all forms of communication are going to be messed up. Also, don't make any big decisions. Mercury affects your ability to think clearly."

"I'll keep that in mind."

"Good. Now, to the aura cleansing." Her voice turned deadly quiet. "This whole 'mango balance' thing is really disturbing me. The island is in shock. Fruit is withering on the trees—just drying up as if the life juices have been sucked out of them."

Pleasant image.

"This is an extremely serious situation," she stressed. "We may not have any mangos for the Festival next weekend, and if we don't, a lot of the growers could end up bankrupt. They depend on the Festival to sell most of their produce."

I clutched the receiver for a few moments, not sure if I wanted to be drawn into her New Age nuttiness. But if something was affecting the mango groves on the island, I guess it qualified as news. "So you think Gina's death is causing this . . . uh . . . imbalance?"

"Absolutely. She was the Mango Queen. The island chose her. She was born here, her father raised mangos, and her grandfather raised mangos. No one could've been a better choice. Mangos are in her lineage."

"I thought a panel of judges picked the Mango Queen." I heard a deep sigh at the other end of the line.

"Mallie, they were guided into making the choice."

"Who could've—"

"The spirit world chose her. *They* guided the judges."

Jeez, Louise. "Okay, let's just say for the moment, that's true. Then the spirit world also chose Brandi as the runner-up, because she's the next rightful Mango Queen. Sort of like the divine right of succession in England."

"Only if Gina's death were from natural causes."

The words reverberated through my head. I clutched the receiver and said nothing.

"All I know is, the spirit world is in turmoil, and it's somehow connected with Gina."

I hated it when she did that. She'd get me all riled up, then refuse to give any specifics. As far as I was concerned, that spirit world was irritating as all get-out. Or maybe it was just that Madame Geri was loony. "Thanks for the tip. We'll know for sure how she died when Detective Billie gets the autopsy results back."

"Mark my words. If her death isn't resolved, the Coral Island mangos will continue to die."

"I'll be certain to pass that on to my temporary editor, Bernice. I'm sure she'll be interested." *When pigs fly,* I added to myself.

"I'll tell her myself when I come in to cleanse your aura tomorrow—"

"No way. My aura is fine. It doesn't need cleansing, buffing, or even refinishing."

"Trust me. I know when an aura needs cleansing." Her voice turned firm, final. "See you in the morning." She hung up before I could answer.

I started to call her back, but then a mental picture rose up in my mind: Madame Geri meeting Bernice. Bonkers vs. Butthead. I smiled. That encounter could potentially cause the earth to reverse its orbit. At the very least, time would stand still for a few minutes, and I'd have more entertainment than I could get from a lifetime of *Seinfeld* reruns.

Still grinning, I read through my story one more time. When I reached the part where I found Gina's body, my smile faded. What was the cause of her death? Maybe Madame Geri was on to something—not that I believed that junk about the spirit world. But something about the way Gina died struck me as unnatural. Sure, it could've been drugs—an overdose. Things like that happened all the time.

But to someone as happy as Gina? The Mango Queen?

It seemed doubtful.

I saved my "Terror on the Trail" story to a flash drive and shut down the computer, my thoughts still on Gina. I'd promised Aunt Lily I'd dig around for information, and, since I still had an obituary to write, it wouldn't be off-limits to talk to Gina's fiancé. Even Detective Billie should understand that—or not.

After checking my notes for Trish and Bryan Palmer's address, I headed toward Sea Belle Isle Point. Located on the southern tip of the island, it was the farthest point away from the Twin Palms RV Resort, where I resided. No doubt the planners of this exclusive community had had that in mind when they built it. They wouldn't want their luxurious residences anywhere near trailers, fifth-wheelers, or, in my case, antique Airstreams. Too low-end. Some of the commonness might rub off.

Each of the Sea Belle Isle Point houses sat on half an acre of carefully manicured land. No wild bougainvillea bushes or spreading sea grape here, thank you very much. The name of the game was control and order. Wide canals stretched behind the houses, with huge boats docked at attention. Rarely used, they provided status for the owners.

I could almost feel horrified, surgically enhanced faces peering out of windows, riveted on Rusty's offensive exterior as we crept down Hibiscus Court, looking for the Palmer residence. Okay, my truck wasn't a Lexus, a Cadillac, or even a high-end Buick. But it was reliable and could pull a 4,225-pound Airstream. I'd like to see anyone try that with one of those fancy cars.

I scanned the mailboxes one by one, then slammed on the brakes as I almost passed the Palmers' mail receptacle. It wasn't one of your run-of-the-mill mailboxes with a wooden base and rounded container at the top. This elaborate contraption resembled a dolphin, its body curving up from the ground, mail-slot "mouth" agape and sealed by a hinged door. Presumably, the mail was shoved in there. *Cute.*

I pulled into the driveway and slid out of my truck, straightening my flamingo T-shirt with a defiant tug. Following the tiled walkway toward the front door, I took in the magnificence of the house. Two-storied, Spanish style, with arches and curved tile on the roof, it puffed up as proudly as the proverbial peacock—a testament to money and power. My mother would love it, which meant I hated it.

As I reached the front screen door, the automatic sprinklers erupted with a stream of sulfur-smelling water. I jumped back, but not before I was drenched from head to toe. *Great. Just great.* I shook the water out of my curls and wiped down my arms and legs. There was nothing I could do about the water spots on my T-shirt and jeans. They'd have to dry in their own time.

Raising my head high, I opened the screen door and strolled down a narrow, enclosed entrance area. I rang the doorbell. Instantly I heard dogs barking from within. I shrugged. Maybe the Palmers weren't so bad after all. If they were dog people, they had to have some redeeming qualities.

The glass-etched front door swung open, and out came two huge German shepherds, teeth bared, advancing on me with woman-eating eyes.

I was done for.

Chapter Nine

Slowly, I backed up, my Birkenstocks heel to toe, making silent contact on the tile. "Good doggies. I've got one of my own, you know—a nice little teacup poodle." The image of Kong's sweet brown eyes and moppet face appeared in my mind. It occurred to me that those features might be the last things I remembered before my life was taken by these two growling hounds from hell.

"Naomi, Neelum, stay!" a forceful masculine voice ordered.

Instantly, the dogs stopped in their tracks, still keeping a wary eye on me.

Poised inside the front door stood a handsome, middle-aged man with one of those tawny George Hamilton tans that bespoke many hours on the beach or in a tanning booth. It was the same guy who'd dropped Gina and Brandi off at the Little Coral Island trail—Brandi and Brett's dad.

"Mr. Palmer?" I asked, edging around the watchful canines.

"It's dangerous to wander into someone's house. Didn't you see the doorbell outside the screened porch?" His thick silver eyebrows slanted downward like two arrows aiming for his nose.

"No, sorry." I reached inside my canvas bag and pulled out one of my cards. I held it out as if it were a talisman. "I'm Mallie Monroe from the *Observer*."

"A reporter?" His tone turned nasty. "You're not welcome here."

"If I could just have a few minutes." I'd almost made it around the devil dogs. "I'm writing an obituary on Gina Fernandez, and I need some information—"

"Don't move; the dogs are trained to kill!" he exclaimed.

The dogs tensed and growled low in their throats. I, too, tensed.

Dry-mouthed, heart pounding, I now knew how postal workers and meter readers felt when they had to enter dog-patrolled territory to do their jobs. At least if I had a mail sack, I'd have something to fight off those monstrous teeth that looked the size of those in a prehistoric dinosaur display. My canvas bag provided only minor protection.

"Weren't you on the trail hike yesterday?" His frown lifted a fraction.

I nodded vigorously, still not daring to speak.

"You were with Brandi . . . and Gina." He paused, no doubt weighing the pros and cons of letting a disheveled journalist into his house. Pro: he'd find out what happened on the trail yesterday. Con: his daughter was one of the last people to see Gina alive.

I waited.

"I'll give you ten minutes." He mumbled something in a foreign language to the dogs. They scrambled away from me and sat down.

Taking in a deep breath, I squared my shoulders and moved toward him with a pseudo-confident step. "No-good mutts," I muttered under my breath.

"Pardon me?"

"I said . . . 'Good little dogs.' "

His features relaxed into a glow of pride. "They're from a special drug-sniffing bloodline and are trained to sniff out terrorists on a dime."

"A useful quality for Coral Island." *Duh.* The worst transgression to hit last week's section of Crimebeat in the *Observer* was some drunk guy pedaling down Cypress Drive in a vinyl poncho—and nothing else. *Big deal.*

"You never know where criminals are hiding." His mouth tightened as he motioned me in. Then he uttered another foreign phrase to Nucklehead and Numnutts, and they trotted off to another part of the house. Hopefully, somewhere with a cage.

"They have interesting names." My sandals squished on the pristine, shiny white tile.

"Naomi and Neelum are types of mangos. The Naomi is a new variety grown in Israel—big and bright red. The Neelum has been around for a while. It's raised mostly in India and China—smallish and bright yellow. No blush. Cuts well into cubes."

"Sounds delicious. I was never a big mango fan till I tried some yesterday and—"

"You don't like *mangos*?" Shocked disbelief threaded through his words. I felt as if I'd said something un-American.

"*Didn't.* Past tense. I've reconsidered my position since I tasted a Coral Island mango."

"I should think so." He led me into a step-down, plushly carpeted, white-on-white living room—the kind that was supposed to look very high class but always made me think of hospital rooms. Sterile and colorless.

"Have a seat." He pointed at an overstuffed, ivory leather sofa. I sank into it, hoping my damp jeans wouldn't leave stains on the cushions.

He remained standing, which was, no doubt, a power play. I

rose to my feet again. Then he seated himself in a matching leather armchair. I slid down into the Jell-O sofa once more.

"So, what do you want to know about Gina?" His hands rested on his upper thighs, palms flat, but the fingers curled into his neatly pressed trousers. "She was engaged to my son, Brett, and that's about all there is to it."

I reached into my canvas bag and pulled out my notepad. "Did she know Brett long?"

"They grew up together on the island but, of course, went to different schools. Brett attended private academies on the East Coast."

"So they were childhood sweethearts?"

"I'd hardly call them that. Passing acquaintances, maybe. They weren't in the same . . . social circles, you could say."

Yeah, I'd say that.

"When Gina did a decorating job on our neighbor's house last year, she and Brett got reacquainted and began to date." He said the last word as if it were an expletive, biting out the last consonant.

"And she was good friends with Brandi, too, from what I saw yesterday."

"I guess so. They were both involved in that Mango Queen thing." He leaned forward, elbows on his knees. "How is any of this relevant to her obituary?"

"I need facts about her life. This won't be a brief obituary, since she was an island girl and the Mango Queen to boot. It'll probably be a half page, so I need a lot of . . . details."

An expression of distaste crossed his features. "I don't want my family put through any more trauma. Please keep us out of the 'details' as much as possible."

"I'll try, but Brett *was* her fiancé." Was Bryan Palmer concerned about his family? Or did he have something to hide? He seemed as tense as a horse straining at the start line.

Maybe I'd jiggle his gate a little. "Let's see now. . . ." I flipped through my notepad. "You dropped off Gina and Brandi at the trail yesterday. Had you met them at Mama Maria's? I know they had breakfast there in the morning."

His eyes narrowed, but then he flashed a smile of white teeth again. Against his tan, they blazed in all their neon glory. "I had breakfast with them."

I made a mental note to check that with Mama Maria. "Was Brett with you?"

"No, he had an early meeting with a client. He's an attorney, you know."

"And Gina was . . . just a decorator," I couldn't resist adding.

"What are you getting at, Ms. Monroe?" The smile vanished.

"It's well known that you didn't like the fact that your son was engaged to Gina. After all, her grandfather was a migrant worker."

"Just because her grandfather worked for my father doesn't mean a thing. She was a lovely girl. And Brett—"

"Her grandfather worked for your family?"

"In our mango groves. We have over a hundred acres cultivated on the island," he revealed with obvious pride. "The land's been in my family for three generations."

"How nice."

He pushed himself to a standing position. "I think I should inform you that the Palmer family has quite a bit of influence on this island, including that little rag of a newspaper you work for. And if you impugn my family's reputation in any way, I'll slap a lawsuit on you faster than—"

"Dad, what's going on?" A slim, young man with patrician features and close-cropped brown hair appeared.

"Nothing, son. Just having a little talk with Ms. Monroe."

"Mallie." I stretched out my hand and moved toward him. "I work at the *Observer.*"

He shook it. "Aren't you the one who . . . found Gina?"

I nodded, noticing the red-rimmed eyes. At least one person in this family was sorry that Gina had died.

"She didn't suffer in any way, did she?" His voice cracked as he asked the question.

"Not from what I could tell—"

"There's no point in speculating," Bryan broke in, placing a hand on his son's shoulder. "You don't want to torture yourself needlessly."

He pulled away. "Dad, my fiancée is dead. You got it? She's the one woman I've ever loved, and I'll never see her again." His eyes filled with tears. "I can't imagine going on without her. . . ." He slid into a chair and dropped his head into his hands.

Bryan's only response was a tightening of his features. "You'll have to excuse my son—he's not himself."

Annoyance rose up inside of me like a jagged burn. "Anyone would be upset at such a loss. I think you need to cut him some slack—"

"Mind your own business. This is *my* family, Ms. Monroe. And we don't need your interfering in matters that don't concern you. My son is my concern—"

"Dad. Will you shut up!" Brett lurched to his feet and glared at his father.

"Brett, I'm only trying to help."

"Well, you're not. You never liked Gina. I knew it, and she knew it. Oh, you pretended all right. But inside, you never accepted her, and I'll never forgive you for that." He shoved past his father and stumbled out of the room.

Bryan Palmer turned to me, his face thunderous. "See what you started? I want you out of this house, *now.*"

A tall, matchstick-thin woman appeared. As deeply tanned as Bryan, she nonetheless hadn't fared so well in the wrinkle department. Deep lines fanned out from her eyes in spite of the unnaturally taut facial skin. Undoubtedly, she'd had plastic surgery, but it hadn't erased the sun damage—just stretched it out like leather over a drum.

I vowed to up my SPF to the highest level known to humankind.

"Darling, please keep your voice down. We don't want the neighbors to hear." She looked at me with wary green eyes. "I'm Trish Palmer."

"Mallie Monroe from the *Observer*. I didn't mean to upset anyone, but I'm working on Gina Fernandez's obituary." Eying her immaculate ivory silk top and skirt, I looked down at my T-shirt and jeans. They were almost dry but still sticking to my skin in some spots.

Her eyes darkened momentarily. From grief? Or something else? "I don't think we can help you much. Our son was engaged to Gina, but we didn't know her all that well."

"But she grew up on Coral Island, and her mother runs one of the most popular restaurants. Surely you were more than passing strangers."

Trish's face assumed a mask of patronizing graciousness, including a phony smile and thin, arched eyebrows. "Of course we were more than strangers. I simply meant we didn't know any . . . intimate details about Gina's life. You'll need to speak with her family for that kind of information."

"Could I talk to Brandi?"

"I don't think that's a good idea." Her voice was soothing, gentle. "She is very upset right now. Perhaps in a few days—"

"Forget it," her husband cut in. "And forget trying to talk with Brett; he won't want to be interviewed—ever. That chapter of his life is closed, and there's no point in making him relive it through memories he needs to put behind him."

"Gina just died yesterday." *Creep.*

Trish moved to position herself between her husband and me.

"You'll have to excuse my husband. Our whole family is still in shock, Ms. Monroe. We each deal with grief in our own way."

Yeah, I've seen more grief over roadkill.

"Let me show you out," Trish continued. Grasping my arm in a surprisingly firm grip, she steered me toward the front door. "Come back in a day or two when we've had a chance to calm down. Then we'll have a statement for the paper." She gave me an encouraging little pat on the shoulder, swung open the front door, and whisked me out in one smooth motion.

I found myself standing in the screened walkway, the front door closed behind me. Talk about the bum's rush. Did I get that treatment out of their grief? Or was it my shabby appearance?

I shoved my notepad into my canvas bag and let myself out of the screened area, keeping a close watch on those oscillating sprinklers. When they arched the farthest away from me, I dashed for my truck. Just making it in time, I closed the door. Unfortunately, I hadn't rolled up the window, and I took another hit of sulfur water in the face—one last indignity before I lit out of there. Obviously, I was not welcome at Sea Belle Isle Point and never would be. Bryan and Trish Palmer had made that very clear. Almost too clear. As if they had something to hide. But what?

I cranked up Rusty and headed for Mango Bay. I needed the comfort and security of my Airstream. I needed to hug my teacup poodle and have him look at me with adoration. Most of all, I needed a shower to get rid of this darn sulfur smell that now clung to me like a used match.

I took one last look at the Palmer house. Bad vibes all around. I drove off.

As I approached my shiny silver Airstream, I took in a deep, cleansing breath. The site was exactly as I had left it. My blue and white striped awning flapped in the slight breeze coming in off the Gulf. My picnic table was positioned underneath, my beach paraphernalia stacked neatly to one side. *Ah, home.*

I eased out of Rusty, and my moment of nirvana dissolved. A blast of yet more Rolling Stones geezer rock assailed my ears. *Ugh.*

Yanking open Rusty's door, I strode over and beat on the side of the aging RV next door. "Turn the music down!"

Laughter erupted from inside yet again.

I rapped on the yellowed siding once more. "I'll call the maintenance guy, and he'll *make* you turn it down."

More laughter. *Okay, I'd probably laugh at that one too.*

They'd probably met Pop Pop Welch and knew he was about as much of a threat as a toothless guard dog—a fitting metaphor, since he rarely remembered to put in his dentures.

I kept banging on the RV with both fists.

Finally, the occupants lowered the music.

I headed back to my Airstream, muttering to myself. First chance, I was going to call Wanda Sue and insist that she get hard-nosed with those dippy, aging hipsters. If she had to hook a stun gun onto Pop Pop's cane, those people were going to abide by the Twin Palms RV rules—or else.

As I was reaching for my door, a tall blond guy in Hawaiian-print swim trunks approached from the beach.

A huge grin spread across my face. "Cole!" I ran toward him.

He swept me up in his arms and spun me around, both of us laughing.

"Hiya, babe." He planted a long, lingering kiss on my mouth. *Wow.*

Chapter Ten

For a few minutes, I reveled in the kiss. My arms slipped around Cole's neck, my feet barely touching the ground. All of my senses sprang to life with a surge of excitement. Heart pounded. Toes tingled. Tremors shot through me. It all felt so familiar and so right.

Eventually, he pulled back and set me on my unsteady feet. We stared at each other, grinning madly. I reached up and brushed back the tendril of blond hair that fell across his forehead—something I always used to do. He caught my hand and kissed the fingers—something he always used to do. I sighed happily.

"I've missed you." So much for playing it cool. But looking at his tawny gold hair, boyish features, and psychedelic-orange board shorts, I was totally caught up in his surfer-dude good looks. Cole was an open book. Nothing hidden. Nothing held back—unlike Nick Billie.

"I've missed you too." He dropped another swift kiss onto my more-than-willing lips.

I placed my hands against his chest to steady myself. "When did you get in? I wasn't expecting you for a while yet. I mean, I thought you were still working on that wildlife-refuge gig in New Mexico. Speaking of that, I loved the postcard you sent. It reminded me of all the times we'd drive to Daytona Beach and soak in the sun, even though I couldn't really get any rays. Remember how I'd have to cover up with pants, shirt, hat, and sunblock? Oh, last year I discovered a new block with this incredible SPF. It really helps so I don't get a zillion new freckles every time—"

Cole began laughing.

"What? What?"

"Same old Mallie. That motormouth hasn't slowed down one bit."

"It must be genetic. Unless they come up with an anti-motormouth medication, I'm pretty much going to be a lost cause."

"I wouldn't say that." His soft blue eyes twinkled.

"You know, I should be mad at you. It's been over two years since you left to 'find yourself.'"

The twinkle dimmed. "I sent postcards."

"Not much of a substitute."

"I know." His voice turned regretful. "I'm sorry, Mallie. I was all kinds of stupid to leave you like that in Orlando. But things were getting heavy between us, and I didn't know how to handle it. I'd never felt that way about anybody before, and it scared the hell out of me. So I took off . . . but I never got you out of my mind."

"Too bad I can't say the same." I toyed with his T-shirt. "I forgot you the moment I met Mickey."

He tensed. "You found another guy?"

"Oh, yeah. He was waiting in the wings for you to leave." I

was enjoying the look of dismay on his face. "A small guy, with whiskers and little white gloves. I saw him at work every day at the Magic Kingdom."

"Huh?"

"Mickey. As in the Mouse?"

Realization dawned on him, and his mouth quirked up on one side. "Okay, I deserved that." Cole flashed me a sheepish look. "If not forgiven, at least I wasn't forgotten, huh?"

"Not completely." My motormouth might still run, but my heart was parked in a lower gear. "A lot has happened since the last time I saw you. I . . . I'm a different person now."

"Is there . . . anybody else in your life?"

"Could be." Now, why did an image of Nick Billie flicker in the back of my mind? It wasn't as if we'd ever even gone out on a date.

"Now, I *am* getting worried—"

A small scratching sound interrupted him.

Cole inclined his head. "You still have Kong?"

"Is the Pope Catholic?"

"Silly me."

I extricated myself from his embrace and opened the door to my Airstream. Kong leaped out as if he were a heat-seeking canine missile, and I caught him. He licked my face with lavish adoration.

"Hiya, Kong," Cole greeted him.

My teacup poodle's ears immediately perked up. He turned his stubby snout and sniffed. Apparently, he remembered Cole, because he began to treat him to the same vigorous tongue worship.

"Traitor," I teased.

Cole rubbed Kong's apricot furry head. "Loyal pooch."

I couldn't help smiling at two of my favorite males. "Where are you staying?"

"Right next door." He pointed at the previously empty spot on the other side of my Airstream. I'd been so preoccupied with my close-encounter-of-the-unpleasant-kind at the Palmer house, I hadn't even noticed the small, neatly kept van conversion parked in the adjacent site.

"Cozy."

"It can't compete with your Airstream, but I call it home." He patted the silver hull of my RV. "How 'bout I treat you to lunch, and we get caught up?"

"Sure . . . no, wait, I can't. I have to interview Mama Maria."

"Who?"

"She's Gina Fernandez's mother. Yesterday I found Gina dead under Old Blacky—a mangrove tree at the entrance to the Little Coral Island trail—and I have to write her obituary because I work for the *Observer.* That's the island paper. My boss' sister is the temporary editor, and I'm really under all kinds of pressure to write a sensationalized story, but I refused—"

"Whoa. You need to fill me in slowly. It's been a long time."

"Sure. Perhaps I can give you the condensed version on our way to Mama Maria's. Let me give Kong a quick walk, take a shower, and then we can drive over to her restaurant together."

"You're on, babe." He touched my face. "The shower would be especially nice. I hate to tell you this, but you smell like a matchbook. Weird."

"Sulfur sprinklers."

"Huh?"

"Never mind." In spite of my stinky state, my heart sang out. Just for now, I wanted to forget about Gina's death. Forget about Bernice the Butthead. Forget about the callous Palmer family.

Cole was back.

In ten minutes, we were zipping along Cypress Road, the main drag of Coral Island. I'd showered, fluffed up my curls, and dressed in a fresh white cotton blouse, fresh jean cutoffs, and my best pair of Birkenstocks. *Not bad.*

"It's nice to see you're still driving Rusty." He patted the faded dashboard. "I've got a lot of good memories connected with this ol' truck."

"Oh, yeah. My personal favorite was when he broke down during that tropical storm in Orlando, and we had to walk four miles in the pounding rain."

"Just an inconvenience." He waved a hand dismissively.

"It took me two days to dry out."

"But you looked pretty cute with your curls all wet and tangled—like a sea nymph."

Heat broke out across the back of my neck. I rolled down my window even farther. *Time to change the subject.* If Cole intended to stay for any length of time, I'd need to get Rusty's air conditioner fixed pronto, or I'd be in a state of constant semi-meltdown.

"So what's been happening in your life, babe?"

I put my motormouth into high gear and filled him in on my job (elevating it a little), the murder cases I'd been involved in (downplaying them a little), my new friends (no embellishment needed), and my Tae Kwon Do skills (*lots* of embellishment needed).

"Who's this Detective Billie?"

"Uh . . . just the local chief deputy."

"You seem to run into him a lot," he observed matter-of-factly.

"Only when I'm working on investigative stories." I felt a blush rising to my cheeks. "And maybe at Town Hall meetings, or the Circle K when we're both getting our morning fix of Krispy Kremes. And maybe—"

"Whoa. Now I *really* am getting worried. Sounds like I've

got some competition in the field, and he's got the home advantage."

I couldn't resist a smile. "Our relationship is strictly professional. He tries to solve his cases; I interfere and drive him crazy."

"Ouch." Cole winced, as though punched in the stomach. "It's worse than I thought. Anytime a woman drives a man crazy, he's interested."

"Male logic?"

"Nope—primitive male instinct. I'd fight him for you, but I'm a pacifist. So I guess I have to cut him out in other, more subtle ways—like by showing you what a responsible guy I've become."

"You're just not the kind of guy who stays." I turned into Mama Maria's parking lot as mixed feelings swirled through me.

A long pause. "Maybe I've changed too."

I didn't respond. Could a leopard change his spots? Could the moon change its orbit? Could Cole become the man of my dreams?

We sat in the truck for a few minutes in silence.

"Let's save this conversation for later, okay?" I finally said. I needed time to take in that Cole was here, and I didn't know how or if he could fit into my life on Coral Island.

He nodded.

I slid out of Rusty and scanned the parking lot. In spite of the trucks and cars lined up in the front spots, a hot, dusty, deserted feeling still surrounded the place.

"Bad vibes." Cole moved to my side.

"Uh-huh." We entered the restaurant. The small dining room seemed more normal than yesterday, with a few patrons and a faint smell of fajitas and tacos. An older couple sat near one of the window tables, talking quietly. Two teenagers occupied the table next to them, both occupied with rapid-fire text-messaging. I didn't know any of them. But seated on one of the stools at the back counter was none other than Everett Jacobs, the island curmudgeon with whom I'd had a couple of run-ins. Cheap and crotchety, he had no relatives and few friends—mainly because he was such a pain in the butt. Sure, he'd sort of saved my life a year ago, but I think he did it more to spite the murderer than to help me.

He turned as we entered, saw me, then just swiveled back around on his stool without saying a word.

"You know him?" Cole asked.

"Yeah," I murmured. "That's another long story. I'll save it for later when we've got the time."

"Go for the short version," Everett tossed off over his shoulder. "When she starts talking, you'll have to wait for the cows to come home before she finishes."

How the heck did he hear me? I approached his aging, bent form, hunched over his coffee cup. "I guess the term 'private conversation' is sort of lost on you, huh?"

He gave a short exclamation of contempt—or maybe he was clearing his throat, ready to spit. I halted and motioned Cole to do the same. My shoes had been the recipients of Everett's expectorate in the past, and it wasn't pleasant.

"Got myself a brand-new pair of hearing aids." He turned around to face us again, pointing at both ears. "And they're on maximum volume. I hear everything now—even stuff that people don't want me to hear. I'm in the catbird seat," he added with a smug smile.

"I can only imagine." Considering how disagreeable he was most of the time, he probably heard the words *old coot* at least a dozen times a day. "This is my friend, Cole."

"Hiya." Cole put out his hand. Everett stared at it for a few seconds, then sighed and reluctantly gave him a slight shake as if he were touching a leper. "Have you lived on Coral Island for long?"

"Long enough to know not to spend time with newcomers."

Cole's friendly demeanor didn't diminish. "I'd think you would want to show people your island and—"

"Too many people here already. The island don't need anybody else."

I rolled my eyes, thinking he couldn't hear *that.* "How's Mama Maria doing?"

Everett's bushy gray eyebrows slanted down in a deep frown. "She's struggling to keep going. I asked her if she needed any help, but she's proud and wants to keep busy so the grief don't eat her alive. Poor lady."

I blinked. Were those words coming out of Everett the Crusty Curmudgeon? Could it be he had a soft side after all?

"So don't go riling her none, missy." He leveled a stern glance at me. "You stick your nose into other people's business for that damn rag of a newspaper and it does nothing but make problems."

That sounded more like the Everett I'd come to know and dislike.

"I have no intention of upsetting her," I declared, wishing it were permissible to kick old men in public. "*She* wanted me to come by today to talk about Gina and gather information for her obituary."

"So that's why you're here." He transferred his eyes to Cole. "What about surfer boy?"

I gritted my teeth. "He's . . . a friend."

Everett scoffed. "This isn't the time for you to be cozying up to some beachcomber, when a lady has lost her daughter."

"Look, Everett, it's none of your business who I spend my time—"

"Mallie, *chica.*" Mama Maria emerged from the kitchen, wearing a black dress and apron. Her eyes still appeared red-rimmed from crying. Her face was sagging with sadness, but she seemed more in control—no broken glass.

She hugged me, and then I introduced her to Cole.

"*Buenos días.* Welcome to our island."

Cole shook hands with her.

"Do you want to take a table?" Mama Maria gestured to a secluded corner of the restaurant.

I touched her arm gently. "We were going to have some lunch, but could I talk to you about Gina first for the story? That is, if you're up to it."

"*Sí.* Come with me." Her mouth tightened into a resolute line, and my admiration for her soared. Every ounce of her strength was being mustered to keep herself from breaking down.

"You two go on," Cole urged. "I'll stay here and have a cup of coffee with my new friend." With a beaming smile, he slapped Everett on the back.

"I've got nothing to say." The old man grimaced.

Cole winked at me as he took the stool next to Everett.

I winked back. Everett might be the most disagreeable man I'd ever met, but Cole was the most agreeable. A battle of wills was about to begin, but I felt confident that my erstwhile boyfriend would come out on top. He had the power of boyish buoyancy. Everett's barbs and jabs would bounce off Cole like sand fleas popping against a porch screen.

I followed Mama Maria out through the kitchen and toward a separate house that was located behind the restaurant. Lush foliage kept the place partially hidden, but behind the bougainvillea bushes, palm trees, and sea grape, I spied a modest-sized, typical Florida cinder block house. It was painted the same bright color as the restaurant and was kept up with the same meticulous neatness.

She didn't speak as she entered the house and led me through a tiled, simply furnished living room, down a hallway lined with family pictures, and into a bedroom.

"This was Gina's room."

I took a moment to look around. I'd met Gina only briefly, so I didn't know quite what to expect. But as I took in the antique four-poster bed, mahogany dresser, and subtle colors of the bedspread and "accent pieces," as my mother would call them, I realized Gina must've been a talented decorator. Certainly, I could've used her help with my Airstream and its mishmash of colors, cheap fixtures, and general lack of any sense of style.

"This is lovely." I ran a hand over the soft green bedspread decorated with tiny palm trees.

She sighed, her eyes tearing up. "Gina could make any room look *bonita*. She redid this whole house and the restaurant after she became a decorator. They came alive. . . ."

But Gina was dead. The words were left unspoken, but we both knew what Mama Maria was thinking.

I strolled around, noticing the framed picture of Gina and Brett on the bedstand—both of them wore huge grins and straw hats as they held up some kind of tropical drinks. They looked so happy.

"That was taken when they were on a cruise earlier this year."

"Nice." What could I say? A pang shot through me at the image of all that youth and happiness. *Gone. All gone.*

On the bed lay a large, thick volume. Mama Maria picked it up and handed it to me. "This was Gina's scrapbook. She kept all her special pictures and favorite fabrics in there, and lots of other things too. I thought you might like to see them."

I sat on the bed and opened the ornate cover. Mama Maria seated herself next to me. As I paged through the scrapbook, she filled me in on Gina's life. Her early years as one of the few Latina girls at the island school, her stint in Miami getting her decorating degree at Florida International University, her partnership with Isabel, her favorite fabric swatches from completed jobs, and, of course, her engagement to Brett. It was all there, in one place—a whole life between the covers of a scrapbook.

"Gina was a very special young woman," I said in a gentle voice as I finally turned the last page.

"*Sí.*" Her head sagged against her chest.

"I'll write the best story I can about her life. I promise you that."

"*Gracias.* She would've liked that." She took in a deep breath and rose to her feet. "Feel free to look around. I'm going back to the restaurant." With slow, halting steps, she headed for the door.

I slid off the bed, clutching the scrapbook against my chest.

Moving around the room, I noticed all the girly items on the dresser: fancy perfume bottles, silver comb and brush, tiny china figurines. Pretty and delicate.

Then, something else caught my eye. Amid the feminine ornaments was a small white box, with a syringe on top.

"Mama Maria, what's this?" I pointed at the box.

She was almost out of the room but turned back. "That was Gina's testing kit. She was a diabetic."

Oh.

Chapter Eleven

How bad was the diabetes? Did she have it long?" I picked up the insulin tester and the syringe and looked them over. That's why the needle was next to Gina's body. She must've been giving herself an insulin shot.

"Since she was a teenager. It came on very sudden, very fast. She almost went into a coma before we could get her to the hospital. But they saved her. Once she got back on her feet, the doctor told her how to check her sugar levels and give herself a shot when she needed it."

"That must've been a pretty hard adjustment to make for someone her age."

Mama Maria shook her head with a tiny smile. "Not for Gina. She saw it as just another challenge. It didn't slow her down one bit."

"Did a lot of people know about it?"

"Only family and a few close friends. She said she didn't want people to pity her."

"But it was serious?"

"Enough to kill her? *Sí.*" A tear slid down one side of her face. "She could get very sick, very fast, if she didn't time her two shots—morning and evening."

"Yet Rivas said—"

"Stupid talk," she muttered with a frown. "Gina was never well. She wouldn't let the disease slow her down, but it always was there, waiting to strike her down. I told her to take things easy, not push herself so hard, but she was stubborn, headstrong. Then, the whole Mango Queen contest stressed her out—she was up all night when she got crowned. And I knew, once she became the Mango Queen, it was just the beginning—she'd have to do things like that stupid trail thing. I think it took her to the limit."

"She seemed pretty lively during the hike," I pointed out.

"Gina put on a brave front. She was not well." Tears started welling up again in Mama Maria's eyes. She shook her head and left the room.

I stared down at the monitor and syringe, my thoughts in a jumble. This revelation put a whole new spin on Gina's death. Was it possible that Aunt Lily and Rivas had let their grief overshadow the very real possibility that Gina's disease had killed her? And why hadn't either of them mentioned it? Wouldn't they have known?

There was one person in particular I needed to share this knowledge with: Detective Nick Billie. With our new relationship based on openness and honesty, I had to get this information to him pronto.

I placed the monitor and syringe in my large canvas bag and exited, allowing myself only one backward glance. The room still seemed to have a sense of Gina's presence. Palpable. Real. And sad.

With a sigh, I moved down the hallway, letting my glance trail down the wall of framed pictures—some in color, some black and white. All different sizes and shapes, they appeared to capture the history of the Fernandez family on Coral Island.

All of a sudden, I stopped. A familiar face stared at me from an old, yellowed photograph. Sure, she was much younger, but there was no mistaking the red hair and freckles: my Great-Aunt Lily. She stood positioned between a Latino man and a young girl who appeared to be about twelve years old. Was that Mama Maria? But who was the man? Maria's father? And why was Aunt Lily in the picture? The photograph emanated an atmosphere of . . . intimacy, almost like that of a family.

Odd.

I glanced down the hall. Mama Maria was already out of sight, Rivas nowhere to be found. I lifted the frame off the wall and slipped it into my bag. *Okay, this is totally illegal.* But I needed to show it to Aunt Lily and find out exactly what her connection was with Mama Maria.

Making my way back to the restaurant, I spotted Cole, who was nodding sympathetically as Everett was pointing at the corns on his left foot.

Poor Cole.

"I've tried everything I can to clear 'em up, but they won't go away. I'm ready to wave a dead chicken over my feet and chant some kind of voodoo spell," Everett grumbled. "My foot aches all the time."

"Try emu oil," Cole suggested. "The stuff works like a miracle. It cured me when I had a pulled muscle."

Everett's bushy gray eyebrows arched upward. "Thanks, sonny. I'll get myself some of that moo oil."

"No, emu oil. *E-M-U.*"

"Come on, Cole." I tapped him on the shoulder. "We need to go—I have to talk to Detective Billie."

"What about lunch?" Cole murmured as he wrote *emu oil* on a napkin and gave it to Everett. "I already ordered tacos for us."

"Maybe we can eat them on the road. I've got to see our island's chief deputy about something urgent."

"Watch her, sonny. She's always up to some kind of mischief. Almost got herself killed a couple of times—she just doesn't know when to back off."

"So I've heard." Cole fastened his blue eyes on me, curiosity and amusement mingled in their depths. "At least life is never dull with a redhead."

"Aw, you'd be better off with a cat—like I have," Everett responded in a disgusted tone. "No fuss. No sissy scenes. And you can get 'em declawed."

Cole grinned. "I think there's a lot to be said for human female claws."

My breath caught at the implication. Did Cole remember those playful nights in Orlando? I hadn't forgotten any of the details, but, then again, having been without a boyfriend for a couple of years, those memories had taken on a cinematic quality.

Just then, the waitress brought our tacos.

"Could you wrap those up to go, please?" I asked.

"Sure thing." She disappeared into the kitchen and reappeared minutes later with the tacos. While Cole paid her, I turned to the old curmudgeon. "It's been real."

He grunted.

"See ya around, Everett." Cole waved at him as we exited the restaurant.

Once outside, I turned toward Cole in awe. "You're incredible. How could you get so friendly with that old coot? I can't stand him. Every time we run into each other, all we do is trade insults."

"You've got to see past all the barriers he puts up," Cole mused aloud. "He's not so bad."

"Everett Jacobs? Hah. Yeats hit the nail on the head when he said an old man is a 'tattered thing.' "

He put an arm around me. "Same old Mallie. Scrapping with the world."

I leaned into his shoulder. "Same old Cole. Surfing through life."

"Yin and yang, babe." He dropped a kiss onto my head. "That's why we're so good together."

We climbed into Rusty, me behind the wheel. "Better open the windows. You know how temperamental Rusty's air conditioner can be."

"Sure do." He handed me a taco, then started in on his own.

I shifted into second gear, noting the sauce dribbling onto my jeans leg. "Darn it."

"Here, let me." Cole took his napkin and dabbed at the stain.

I flashed him a sidelong smile. "How have I made it this long without you?"

"I don't know. Maybe we should remedy the situation."

"Cole, I don't want to be having this discussion while I'm trying to eat a taco, drive my rust bucket of a car, and write Gina Fernandez's obituary."

"Okay . . . later, dudette."

But the words had been spoken. They silently echoed in my mind, creating momentary images of a future that were just too good to be true. Cole and I as a couple again? Was I ready for that?

And what about Nick Billie? An image of his smoky eyes drifted through my mind—sexy and irresistible.

Minutes later, we pulled into the police station parking lot and finished our tacos. A smallish gray structure, built up about six feet on cement blocks, the station always gave the appearance of being the calm center of the island. Neatly landscaped, with white latticework around the base, it was also an immaculate oasis of authority. "Do you want to come in?"

"Wouldn't miss it for the world. I want to meet my rival."

"Detective Billie? I told you, he doesn't even like me." Even though he'd held my hand under the black mangrove tree.

"*Like* has nothing to do with it, babe."

"You're being downright silly," I muttered as I shouldered open my door and hopped out. Was I protesting too much?

My steps faltered, and Cole caught my elbow. "Did you trip on something?"

"Uh . . . maybe a shell." I bent my leg and peered at the bottom of my Birkenstock. "Looks okay. But you never know. Most of the roads and parking lots on the island are made up of crushed shells. The kind you see on the beach. Not that you find too many these days, what with all the tourists and red tide and . . . everything."

He propelled me through the door, whispering, "I must've hit a nerve. Your motormouth just activated."

Damn. He knew me too well.

"Hi, Rhonda," I greeted Nick's superefficient, superattractive, and supernice secretary. "Is Nick in?"

"Sure, just let me buzz him."

She didn't have to. His tall, lean figure appeared in the doorway of his office, arms folded, dark eyebrows raised as he looked from me to Cole and back again. "I was just about to call you. The preliminary coroner's report came in on Gina's death."

"That's why I'm here—Gina. I . . . uh . . . picked up some information about an hour ago that I wanted to share with you." Nervously, I picked over my words. "We'd gone to Mama Maria's for lunch so I could interview her for my story on Gina. One thing led to another, and—"

"Maybe you ought to come into my office." That long-suffering note that I knew so well had entered his voice.

"Sure."

He looked at Cole with pointed curiosity.

"Oh, sorry. This is an old . . . friend, Cole Whitney. He's staying at the Twin Palms for a while."

Awkward pause. Why did I feel so odd introducing him to Nick?

"Glad to meet you." Cole shook his hand with his easy I-just-caught-a-big-wave surfer-guy style. "Mallie has told me a lot about you."

"None of it good, I'll bet."

"Untrue. She respects you a lot."

"Really? You could've fooled me. We've had our share of clashes over the last year, and—"

"No need to go into that," I cut in quickly. Why remind him of all the trouble I'd caused with his last two murder investigations? I felt uneasy enough right now. "We have a good, working, professional relationship. Right?"

A flash of humor crossed Nick's face. "Right."

Rhonda scanned our little group. "Can I get anyone a cup of coffee?"

I shook my head.

"Decaf?" Cole asked.

"Nope, only high-test," Rhonda informed him with a smile.

"Thanks, anyway." Cole smiled back. "I don't do caffeine. The stuff is poison."

"You're a friend of Mallie's?" Nick inquired, disbelief flitting across his face. "Her whole life is caffeine and junk food."

"Not my whole life—just my meals," I said defensively.

Nick shrugged and motioned me toward the inner sanctum. "You'll have to wait out here, Cole. Official police business."

"No problem. I don't mind waiting." He seated himself on

the leather sofa and picked up an old sports magazine. "Take your time."

I moved past Nick, and he closed the door behind me, something he rarely did. "Okay, before I tell you anything, what was the cause of Gina's death?" I asked.

He exhaled audibly as he slid into the chair behind his desk. "Maybe you ought to sit down."

My knees sort of buckled, and I felt the hard leather under me. "Was it . . . murder?"

"Possibly. The coroner found high levels of a deadly pesticide in Gina's blood." His voice had turned flat, his eyes obsidian, as he revealed the news.

I sat back, stunned. "But . . . how?"

"You remember the syringe we found near her body? Traces of the pesticide were in it too."

"When I was with Mama Maria, I found out that Gina was diabetic—a pretty serious case. That's what I was going to tell you. Is it possible she was giving herself an insulin injection and accidentally got some pesticide on the needle?"

"Not likely, considering the amount of the toxin found in her system." He didn't blink at my revelation.

I locked glances with him. "You knew about the diabetes, didn't you?"

"Yes."

Irritation flared inside of me. "Why didn't you share that information rather than let me think she was some kind of drug addict?"

"I couldn't. All personal details are confidential until cause of death is determined." His tone wafted over me like an arctic breeze. *Oh, great*—the chill was back.

I groaned. "Not that old refrain again."

"Mallie, you have to trust my judgment when it comes to sharing information."

"And you have to trust that I can tell the difference between writing a news story and revealing facts that could jeopardize your investigation." My fingers gripped the armrests of the chair.

"Well . . . you know now."

"Days after Gina's death—and no thanks to you." I sniffed in disapproval.

He placed both hands on the desk and folded them with an air of composed superiority. "You want to continue throwing a hissy fit or talk about the case?"

"I feel like we've taken two steps backward. What's happened?"

"Nothing at all." His features assumed a mask as remote as the faces on Mount Rushmore.

What the heck was going on? We were on a first-name basis. We'd held hands under the mangrove tree and talked about life and death. That meant something.

All of a sudden, a thought occurred to me. Was he jealous of Cole? Could it be?

"May I at least have a formal statement from you about Gina's death?" I reached inside my canvas bag for my notepad and pen.

"No comment for the record yet."

"Off the record?" I raised my brows. "Come on . . . I deserve at least that."

"It looks like . . . she was poisoned by the pesticide."

"So that would mean someone put it in Gina's syringe." *How? When?* Thoughts skittered through my brain like cars weaving on a racetrack, distracting me from the whole Cole/Nick jealousy thing. "Mama Maria told me that Gina gave herself two injections a day; that would mean the evening shot from the night before was normal. But the morning shot had to have been tampered with by . . . the killer."

"My thoughts exactly."

"Then, whoever did it knew that Gina was a diabetic and had to have access to her syringe that morning." I brushed a hand across my forehead, sucking in air in breathless realization. "Family and friends."

Nick regarded me in silent agreement.

"Wait a minute. I know her mother and brother were genuinely devastated by her death. They couldn't have done it. And her fiancé, Brett, seemed just as stricken." Dawning realization hit me. "But those potential in-laws—"

"The Palmers?"

I nodded, their suspicious behavior flooding into my brain faster than my motormouth could handle. "When I spoke to Mr. Palmer yesterday, he seemed uneasy, to say the least. And his wife also appeared to be hiding something. And let's not forget that Brandi Palmer had everything to gain from Gina's death. She could finally realize her lifelong dream of becoming Mango Queen—"

"Stop right there. You need to be careful. The Palmers are very influential people on Coral Island, and they could make life unpleasant for you at the newspaper."

"What could be worse than Bernice?" I responded. "Are you saying you're not considering them the prime suspects?"

His mouth hardened. "Based on what? A suspicion that they didn't like their prospective daughter-in-law?"

"That seems like probable cause."

"When you're dealing with rich and powerful people, investigations have to be handled with the utmost delicacy. They have legions of attorneys watching every move of the process. The least little thing that doesn't go by the book can cause a case to be thrown out in the courts."

"The same laws apply to everyone—rich or poor."

"True, but people don't always receive the same treatment—or verdict."

I shook my head. "That stinks. If Gina was killed, those people did it."

"Are you so sure?" he probed. "Rivas wasn't happy about his sister's engagement, and I'd heard rumors that Gina's business partner, Isabel Morales, owed her a lot of money. And there might be other suspects. . . ."

I remembered Rivas' outburst of fury in Mama Maria's kitchen and his hatred of the Palmers. He certainly had the temperament that could lead to murder. But his own sister? I shivered. As for Isabel, who knows?

"Of course, this is all off the record. Until I get the official coroner's report, the cause of death is still indeterminate."

"I assume you mean that's what you want me to put in my story. But I can't do that after everything you just told me." I flipped open my notepad, pen poised in hopeful appeal. "Look, I've got Bernice breathing down my neck to sensationalize my front-page 'Terror on the Trail' piece. I'm trying to hold the line between my journalistic integrity and keeping my temporary editor satisfied, but I've got to have something from you. If Bernice finds out that I'm holding back, I'm out on my ear. So I'm going to ask you again. May I have a formal statement for the record?"

A tiny muscle twitched in his jaw. Then he sighed. "Circumstances point to a suspicious death."

I scribbled his words down on paper. "I'm also doing an expanded obit on Gina, so I'll be discreet as I'm digging for background."

"Just stay away from the Palmers," he warned. "For your sake."

"Okay, but I may need to talk to Brett." I held up my notepad and smiled. "It's nice to know you're concerned about me."

"You do tend to rush in before you've thought things

through. Must be something to do with having hair the color of wildfire."

I resisted tossing my curls. "Life's too short to play it safe."

"That's where we disagree." His expression stilled and grew suddenly intense. "Does your boyfriend feel the same way?"

The air immediately grew charged between us with that strange electricity. "He's not exactly . . . my boyfriend."

"But he was at one time."

"Sort of." I looked down, pretending to write a few more lines so he wouldn't see the truth in my face. Cole had meant a lot to me. After a few minutes, I shut the notepad and tossed it into my canvas bag. "Okay, then, that should do it. I appreciate your time."

"Is he staying with you at the Twin Palms?"

I rose to my feet. "I'm not sure that it's any of your business, but he's in his own van."

"Parked next to your Airstream?"

My head tilted to one side so I could scan his hard-planed face. "If I didn't know better, I'd think you were jealous."

Something flickered in the depths of his eyes.

Ohmygod.

Detective Nick Billie *was* jealous.

Chapter Twelve

I left Nick's office, my mind in a whirl, not able to say much to Cole as I drove him back to the Twin Palms RV Resort. This whole romantic-triangle thing was freaking me out.

I needed some time to think.

Besides, I had a story to write and what appeared to be another murder investigation staring me in the face. Was it possible that my life had become so complicated in a scant few days?

Cole, being Cole, completely understood my need for space. We agreed to have dinner later that night.

Then, I drove slowly back to the *Observer* office, giving myself a little respite to first run through the details of Gina's death. So, it turned out that she was poisoned. Rivas and Aunt Lily had been right when they suspected that her death hadn't been an accident. But how did they know?

Had Rivas been involved in some kind of way?

And what about Aunt Lily?

I remembered the picture I'd taken from the Fernandez house. What was my great-aunt's connection with that family?

I made a mental note to call her as soon as I got to the office and start probing for details.

So, onto the more interesting dilemma of being torn between two men.

The thought of Cole wanting to be back in my life set my heart all atwitter; the thought of reserved, by-the-book island chief deputy, Nick Billie, being jealous of Cole sent me practically into cardiac arrest.

I didn't know what to think. Deep, meaningful relationships were *not* my forte, and neither of the potential boyfriends had exactly committed to me.

I pulled into the strip mall that housed our small office, undecided and dazed.

When in doubt, think about it later. I needed all my focus to survive another day with Bernice the Butthead.

Taking in a deep breath, I entered the office with halting steps.

I looked around to find the office empty. *Yippee.* And then I noticed that the stump was gone. *Double yippee.* That damp, dirt smell had dissipated, but . . . now something else permeated the air.

I sniffed.

It smelled like . . . motor oil. Then I spotted the new addition to the office: some sort of engine with a sign next to it that read CHARLEY'S: CORAL ISLAND'S ONLY FULL-SERVICE GARAGE. *Oh, no.*

"Sandy?" I scanned the office again, a trickle of fear running down my spine. Had Bernice finally pushed her beyond the brink and she'd quit?

"She's out to lunch." Speak of the devil—or, rather, Bernice. And I mean *devil.* Bernice stood in the doorway to her office and looked like hell. Her hair was matted, her eyes redrimmed, her crow's-feet trotting all the way down her cheeks.

"Are you . . . uh . . . okay?"

She rubbed her eyes and forehead. "Haven't you ever seen anyone who's tied one on the night before? Good Lord, I must be getting old. I used to be able to drink anyone under the table. All I had last night was a six-pack, and I can barely hold my head up today—after spending most of the night worshipping the porcelain goddess."

Charming image.

"What have you been up to, Miss Priss?" She slumped into Sandy's chair.

I turned away, stalling for time. "Just working my story on Gina. I interviewed Mama Maria this morning."

"And talked to Nick Billie, right?"

Jeez. How did she find out so fast? Glad that my back was to her, I grasped a few moments to come up with an answer. "He gave me an official statement about Gina's death." I pulled out my notepad and faced her again. Flipping a few pages, I pretended to scan my notes and comment in an offhand manner: "Detective Billie's formal statement was . . . 'suspicious death.' That's all I know."

"Good enough for our purposes—yessiree." She thumped Sandy's desk in excitement with one hand. Then she groaned and placed her palms on either temple. "That was a mistake. My head feels like it's going to explode."

Too bad. Anyone who would take pleasure in Gina's death was beyond compassion, even if she had a megahangover. I slammed my heavy canvas bag onto the desk, noticing that Sandy had left a message for me from Gina's decorating partner, Isabel. The thud reverberated around the room, causing Bernice to groan again. *Hah.*

"Write the obit the way you want, Miss Priss," she managed to get out. "But play up a possible murder angle on the 'Terror on the Trail' story. It's a front-page dream."

"Bernice, how about a little respect? Gina died under suspicious circumstances. I'd hardly call it a *dream*—more like a nightmare."

"It's all a matter of perspective." She flipped open a cola and unwrapped a lollipop. "Sure, murder is a terrible thing, and I sympathize with the family, but I've also got newspapers to sell. The business of life goes on." She slid the lollipop into her mouth.

I had no response to that. Was Bernice a heartless old bag or just a realist?

"Get to work. We've got a deadline to meet tomorrow. Both stories have to be done by then. Chop-chop." She pushed herself upright again and threw a T-shirt at me. "Here, this is from our newest advertiser."

I held it up and rolled my eyes. *Get a Grease Job at Charley's Garage.* Simple and tacky—just like Bernice. "Don't tell me. Charley was your drinking buddy last night."

"Of course." She grinned. "Most business deals are done over meals and, more important, beer."

Just at that moment, Sandy strolled in with her fiancé, Jimmy, and his mother, Madame Geri, the island's freelance psychic. Now it was my turn to grin, especially when I spied Madame Geri's turquoise parrot, Marley, on her shoulder. I could hardly wait for the clash of crazies that was about to take place, so I sat down and tipped my chair forward in anticipation.

"Bernice, I'd like to introduce Madame Geri," Sandy began in a chipper voice. "She writes our astrology column for the paper."

"Are you joking?" Bernice blinked a couple of times as she beheld Madame Geri's appearance: blond dreadlocks, Betty Crocker–style dress, and small cigar-box-style purse. A retro Rastafarian.

"Nope, she's the real deal," I cut in with a jaunty bob of my head. "And she helped me solve a murder last year," I added with a second jaunty bob of my head.

Marley let out a piercing squawk, and Bernice howled and winced as if given an electroshock. She held out her lollipop as if to ward off an evil goblin. "Keep that damn bird quiet—and away from me."

"Marley is not a bird. He's my link to the spirit world," Madame Geri clarified in a calm voice. She then halted about three feet in front of Bernice. They stared each other down. It was quite a sight: a hungover hag facing a New Age nut. But neither backed down.

"This office is sacred space and shouldn't house this kind of junk." Madame Geri pointed at the grease-soaked engine part on the floor. "It's bad karma."

"Says you." Bernice included a rude hand gesture.

Madame Geri ignored both responses. "There are bigger things going on than you realize."

"Okay, I'll bite. Like what?"

Madame Geri raised her chin, keeping Marley close. "The mango balance is off. The island is in mourning for its dead queen."

"Huh?" Bernice's mouth pursed, causing her wrinkles to deepen.

"The island chose its queen," Madame Geri explained, glancing at me with a solemn expression, then back at Bernice. "Now that she's dead, all the mangos are shriveling on the trees, as I told Mallie. Our Mango Festival will have no mangos if the balance isn't restored."

"So?"

"The island's economy depends on the mangos. People will suffer. Your paper will go down because no one will have the money to buy advertisements."

Bernice started. That hit a nerve. *Bravo, Madame Geri.*

"Oh, my, yes. The mango balance must be restored." Madame Geri closed her eyes briefly as if to confirm her pronouncement with the spirit world. I guess it was like tuning into a radio station for the top-forty hits. Once you had the frequency, you got all the tunes.

"What am *I* supposed to do about it?" Bernice said, keeping a wary eye on Marley.

"Let Mallie do her job—unobstructed. She'll find the murderer."

Every eye in the room fastened on me, pinning me to the wall like J. Alfred Prufrock in the Eliot poem. I squirmed just as he did in his mind when "fixed in a formulated phrase." What had gotten into Madame Geri?

"Who said it was murder?" my temporary editor asked.

"I did." Madame Geri stroked Marley. "I was told the day it happened."

"By the killer?" Bernice's face kindled in excitement.

"The spirit world."

"Jeez, spare me," Bernice muttered, throwing her hands up. "This kind of hokum might work with the dimwits who live on this godforsaken island, but I'm not one of them. Mango balance? Don't be ridiculous. It's fruit, you idiot. As for Gina's possible murder, we'll investigate it like any other story."

Madame Geri turned deadly quiet.

"You stick to what you know best: phony astrology predictions. And I'll do what I do best: dig up advertising dollars for this rag of a newspaper." Bernice waved her lollipop in Madame Geri's face.

Marley lifted his wings and let out another loud squawk.

Bernice covered her ears and shrieked: "Keep that thing quiet!"

"Shh. It's okay, my darling." Madame Geri soothed her bird, then handed him to Jimmy, all the while watching Bernice. Then she opened her cigar-box-style purse and pulled out a dainty crystal on a silver chain. She began murmuring in a low voice.

"What the heck are you doing?" Bernice asked, when she finally dropped her hands.

Madame Geri kept up the singsong little chant.

"Uh-oh," Jimmy said. "You're in trouble now."

Bernice transferred her gaze from mother to son. "Get her outta here, will ya?"

"Sorry." He shifted Marley to perch on his arm. "I can't till she's finished with her curse."

"What?"

"Her curse." A touch of awe entered Jimmy's voice. "My mother is putting curse on you."

Sandy and I gasped. Even *I* wouldn't brave that, and I was a nonbeliever in Madame Geri's mystic twaddle.

Madame Geri's curses were well known around the island. When her neighbor, Emmie Samwick, refused to keep her crazy Doberman, Bubba, away from Marley, Madame Geri put a curse on her. Within six weeks, Emmie's roof began to leak, her car broke down repeatedly, and her hair began to fall out in clumps (to be honest, that last one might have been the cheap hair dye). After three months of a leaky roof, nonfunctioning car, and increasingly bald head, Emmie finally relented and chained up Bubba when she was at work.

Presumably, Madame Geri then removed the curse, and all was well. But it was still another month before Emmie's hair was restored to its former glory.

I rolled my chair backward—just to make certain none of the curse wafted in my direction.

Finally, Madame Geri stopped and put away the crystal. "It's done. You'll never know another moment's peace till you set things right again," she warned Bernice.

My foolhardy boss snorted, but I could tell she was secretly a bit shaken. It's not every day you wake up to a hangover and a curse—all in the space of twenty-four hours.

Bernice chomped down on her lollipop. "Ow!" She pulled out the empty stick and then poked at her cheek. "I can't believe it—I think I cracked a crown."

Madame Geri's mouth curved upward.

Leaving Bernice swearing and holding the side of her face, Madame Geri pivoted and sailed out of the office, Jimmy in her wake with Marley.

He blew Sandy a kiss. "See ya later, sweetie."

But Madame Geri had one parting salvo for me before she left: "Mallie, the secret lies in the mangos. That's where it all began, and that's where it will end."

"Secret?" I inquired.

She nodded. "You have to find out what happened to Gina, or the mangos will never ripen again."

"But—" Too late. The island's Oracle of Delphi was gone.

"What a loon," Bernice muttered, flexing her jaw back and forth.

"She is not," Sandy retorted as she skirted the greasy engine and took her place at the desk near mine. "Madame Geri is well respected on this island, and her curses are not to be taken lightly."

"I'm shaking in my shoes." Bernice made her legs quiver in faux fear.

"You will be. The broken crown is just the beginning of the curse." Sandy grabbed a chocolate bar from her drawer and wagged it for emphasis. She started to rip off the wrapper, paused, then thought better of it. Tossing the chocolate back into her desk drawer, she took in a deep breath of self-satisfaction.

"Good for you, Sandy." I gave her a thumbs-up. Madame Geri's curse and Jimmy's support had given her the courage she needed. "You don't need food as a crutch anymore."

"I sure don't—even if I have to smell engine oil and wear crummy clothing promoting 'grease jobs.'" She held up her Charley's Garage T-shirt. "I refuse to take refuge in candy therapy."

"Nothing wrong with a little motor grime," Bernice quipped.

"You have no idea how 'grimy' it's going to get," Sandy promised.

Bernice blurted out an expletive and flung her cracked crown into the trash. "That was just a coincidence." She stomped into her office and slammed the door, but it didn't shut. The hinges popped off, and the whole thing crashed to the floor with a thunderous clatter.

"Holy hell!" Bernice screamed. "My head is splitting!"

Sandy sighed in contentment.

Talk about Madame Geri magic!

Humming to myself, I went back to work. Two hours later, I'd placed the final touches on the "Terror on the Trail" story and finished my obituary on Gina Fernandez. Maybe the engine-oil odor had actually inspired me, but I'd never written articles that quickly. Or maybe it was the continual cursing coming out of Bernice's office as her stapler broke, her chair leg cracked, and her computer went down. *You go, Madame Geri.*

I set the hard copies on Bernice's desk, chitchatted for a few minutes, and wished her a good evening, knowing her hell had just begun.

Doing a joyful little dance all the way back to my desk, I began to pack up, noting that Sandy had just finished printing out several pages on the creaky laser-jet printer.

"After what Madame Geri said, I decided to research the *Observer* archives for any information relating to mangos on Coral Island." She handed me a small stack of articles. "The last reporter who was here did a series on the history of growing mangos on the island."

"The one who went berserk in the Dairy Queen drive-through?"

Sandy nodded. "She wasn't a bad writer."

"I'll bet." I shoved my notepad into my bag. "I'm going to swing by Island Décor and see what Isabel wanted."

"Wait." She shuffled through the afternoon mail. "With all the upheaval going on, I forgot that this letter came for you."

She handed me a legal-sized manila envelope. I opened it and shook out the contents on her desk. "What's this?" It looked as if someone had taken a photo and cut it into pieces.

Sandy shuffled the fragments into a semblance of the original picture. Her hand went to her mouth. "Cripes! This is the picture of *you* that ran in the *Observer* when Anita hired you."

A cold chill snaked through me.

Someone had sliced up my picture—and made sure I saw it.

On the short drive to Island Décor, I tried to rationalize a motivation for the cut-up photograph.

People got ticked off with reporters all the time. This was a small island, and I was the main reporter for the *Observer,* so I took most of the flak.

Right from the beginning of my employment at the newspaper, readers had called and complained about my stories—like the one on the bike path. One reader felt I was too "pro bike," and another one felt I was too "anti bike." Then there were the usual gripes about media bias—blah, blah, blah.

This was probably nothing more than a disgruntled *Ob-*

server subscriber who posed no more of a threat than Everett Jacobs the Curmudgeon.

What about the hang-up phone calls?

My sweaty hands clenched the wheel. So much had happened today, I'd forgotten about the calls. Was is possible that whoever was calling me and hanging up had decided to kick it up a notch and send me a perverse, Picasso-like version of my picture?

But who?

The only stories I was working on right now were those connected with Gina Fernandez's death—or, rather, murder.

My nerves tensed tighter than a guitar string tweaked for an evening's performance. Someone didn't like my sniffing around for information about Gina. And that someone could be her killer—maybe even a person I'd already questioned in regard to her death.

I ran through a list of whom I'd talked to in the last two days.

Rivas—the angry brother. He certainly had the temperament to kill but a doubtful motive.

Brandi—the rival for Mango Queen. She had motive, that's for sure. But was she a killer?

Trish and Bryan Palmer—the snobby potential in-laws. They seemed to hate Gina for having the audacity to become engaged to their son, Brett. But was that a motive for murder?

Isabel Morales—the business partner who owed Gina money. Could she have been so desperate that she wanted to wipe clean the debt by eliminating having to pay it back?

My thoughts raced from one suspect to another like a frenzied hamster on a wheel, spinning around and around and around. But the constant mental motion produced no answers. I took in a deep breath and exhaled, trying to settle my mind. That cut-up picture had shaken me, that's for sure.

Keep it together. Isabel was waiting for me.

I pulled into the parking lot of Island Décor and did my "mugatoni" chant for a few minutes. I wasn't sure if it helped or not, except that it sparked a sudden hunger for spaghetti.

As I entered, the door chime tinkled, and the vanilla scent wafted toward me. It was certainly better than the smell of dead fish or engine oil at the newspaper office. Maybe I could persuade Isabel to advertise with the *Observer,* so we could finally have a pleasant odor to counteract Bernice's stinky clients.

"Thank goodness you came." Isabel came rushing toward me, her dark hair flying behind her. I spied the wildness in her eyes and heard the panic in her voice. Something was obviously very wrong.

"What's happened?"

"I have to show you. Come into the back room." She led me past the flowered-chintz sofa, the delicate armchairs, the carefully placed bronze ornaments, and the flowery artwork toward the back room. When we entered, I found myself taking a step back in surprise. Unlike the carefully arranged front room, this space was cluttered from top to bottom with fabric and boxes of assorted sizes. In the middle stood an oak rolltop desk.

"There." Isabel pointed at the desk.

I scanned the messy top. It looked like the rest of the room. "Is there something amiss?" *An understatement.*

"I'll say." She gave an exclamation of impatience. "That's Gina's desk. She was a neat freak. Not a single paper was ever out of order."

"It certainly doesn't look very tidy now." Order forms and papers were strewn every which way.

"My point exactly—it was organized until today." She hugged her arms around herself in a protective stance. "Someone was in here between the time I left yesterday, at around five, and this morning."

"Any sign of forced entry?"

She grimaced. "No, but a good wind could blow open that back door. We kept meaning to get it fixed, but we just never got around to it."

"Was anything stolen, from what you could tell?"

"Uh . . . no. I did a quick inventory this morning, and everything appears to be here, including all of our pricey antiques, expensive knickknacks, and artwork. Nothing's missing. That's why I didn't call the police. How could I tell Detective Billie that someone came into the place and messed up Gina's desk? I'd sound like a fool."

"Maybe not." *Especially with the latest information on Gina's death,* I added to myself.

Isabel's whole face crumpled into an expression of despair. "Why did all of this happen?"

"That's what I'm trying to find out." I looked down at the desk and debated what to do. Considering this was a potential crime scene, Detective Billie would kill me if I got fingerprints anywhere on Gina's desk. "Could you get me a pencil with an eraser?"

"Sure. But . . . why?" She produced one.

"Reporter's tool." *He's still going to kill me. I shouldn't be doing this.* I edged aside the papers with the eraser tip and sorted through them, shoving the letters into one pile and the green order forms into another. The letters were just short notes, saying when a certain item would arrive or confirming a fabric change. But the order forms listed every recent item Island Décor had provided for its clients. I sifted through them as best I could by date. "Did you usually have an order going out every day?"

Isabel began to cry softly.

"I know this is hard for you, but I need you to try to hold it together."

She swiped the back of her hand across her face and sniffed. "Uh . . . yeah, we usually had orders going out every day."

"How were they delivered?"

"If they were big-ticket items, our handyman would deliver them. Gina or I would drop off smaller pieces. Then, afterward, we'd stamp the invoice and file it."

An idea began to germinate inside of me as I flicked my trusty eraser head through the order forms again. There appeared to be a form for every day during the last two weeks—except the day Gina died.

"Was she delivering anything that morning of the trail hike?"

Isabel's tear-filled eyes met and held mine. "I . . . I don't know. Maybe." She shook her head. "I just can't remember right now. My brain isn't working on all cylinders."

"I understand." I turned away from the desk with a resigned shrug. Then I noticed a small laptop computer under a pile of fabric. My breath quickened as I eased the slim orange MacBook from under the stack of tropical cottons and handed it to her. "I don't suppose you cross-filed your hard-copy orders on this laptop?"

"No—sorry. We kept saying we were going to install a computer system for our inventory, but we never got around to it—just like fixing the back door. We always thought there would be time." She brushed her fingers across the neon surface of the laptop. "This was Gina's personal computer."

Another dead end. "Still, there might be something on it that we could use. If you could do a quick run-though of her files, you might find something useful."

"I guess so." Her voice sounded as hopeful as a sigh lost in the wind. "I'll give it a shot."

"You also need to call Detective Billie—just to play it

safe." I set the pencil on the desk between the two paper stacks. He'd know what I'd done. There was no point trying to hide it. The man saw everything.

She nodded, clutching the laptop to her chest. "Do you think someone took the invoice?"

"Maybe."

Dawning recognition widened her still-teary eyes. "That means the intruder might be a client of ours."

We hugged for a few moments, and then I left. I climbed into Rusty, leaned my head against the steering wheel, and closed my eyes.

The phone calls, the cut-up picture, the missing invoice. It all added up to one thing: the killer was getting worried—and maybe ready to strike again.

Yikes.

Chapter Thirteen

By the time I had pulled into the Twin Palms RV Resort on Mango Bay, I felt slightly more composed. Or maybe I was just numb from the mixture of recent events and the stifling heat in my truck. Even with the windows cracked and the air-conditioning (such as it was) blasting valiantly, I was pretty much drenched with sweat from the short, fifteen-minute ride.

But the sight of my gleaming silver Airstream put a smile onto my face. There was something so reassuring about that 4,225-pound antique trailer. I could take anything as long as I had my Airstream—and Kong, my teacup poodle. Oh, and my mugatoni meditation.

I parked Rusty alongside the Airstream and climbed out, ready for a blast of oldies rock from the tenement on wheels next door.

Nothing—just blessed quiet.

Goody.

As I came around the front of my Airstream toward the awning, I spied an unbelievably welcome sight. My rough, sun-faded picnic table had been covered with a white linen tablecloth. Two large candles held it down on either side, and fresh hibiscus flowers were scattered around, lending a splash of scarlet color. Paper plates and paper napkins completed the elegant table setting.

"Hiya, babe!" Cole waved a pair of tongs in my direction. He stood off in the sandy area, next to a barbecue. "How was your day?"

"Weird."

"I figured that. You take a shower, get comfortable, and let the Cole-man take care of dinner. I'm grilling some fresh grouper and veggies. Baked potatoes are in the microwave. Oh, and I walked your minuscule mutt."

"Wahoo. But watch the 'tiny' dog talk—he's got size issues," I joked, trying to cover my mixed emotions. Many a time when we'd lived in Orlando, this very scene would play out after I'd spent a hard day of trying to be a professional on one of my many pre–Disney World jobs. Needless to say, I don't do "professional" well.

"You okay?" Cole asked. His blond hair glinted in the late-afternoon sunlight.

"Sure." This was all so familiar—too familiar. And comfortable—too comfortable. Cole had been gone a long time, and I wasn't sure exactly where he fit into my life right now. "Gimme a few minutes."

"Just a few. Your Great-Aunt Lily called, and she's coming over with somebody named Sam."

"Tonight?" In spite of my fatigue, I perked up. Maybe I could get some answers out of her about the photo I had found at Mama Maria's house.

"She was very insistent."

"It's all right." I pushed back my curls from my sweaty forehead. "You've never met her, have you?"

He shook his head.

I smiled. "You're in for a treat." Opening the door to my Airstream, I was greeted by an apricot fluff ball cannoning toward me, barking rapidly as though he hadn't seen me in a year. "Good dog—even if you are a minimutt."

He barked again.

I needed a shower. Then I could put the day into perspective and ready myself to talk with Aunt Lily. The Cole thing would have to wait. I couldn't even begin to analyze how I felt about having him here, maybe taking up where we'd left off in Orlando.

"Kong, why does everything have to be so complicated?" Nuzzling his tiny black nose, I carried him into the bathroom. I stripped down and enjoyed a long, long, cool shower, soaping and shampooing with extra relish. The heat just poured off me and, with it, some of my fatigue.

Afterward, I fluffed my red curls, dressed in a fresh pink T-shirt (with no advertising slogan), and white Capris. Not exactly dinner garb but, for Coral Island, almost formal attire.

Now I could at least think straight.

First, a snack to tide me over. I opened the fridge, spied some of the mango slices left over from the trail hike, and nibbled on them, leaving a small piece for later. *Yum. Manna from heaven.*

Fortified, I reached into my canvas bag for the framed picture I'd swiped from Mama Maria's, careful not to break the glass. I studied it for a few moments, marveling at how much the young Aunt Lily looked like me.

Genetics, I guess.

Then I focused on the other two people. The young girl had to be Mama Maria—her features were unmistakable. But the Latino man was a mystery. Her father? Slightly taller than Aunt Lily, he stood proudly with his shoulders squared and chin high. He had dark hair, a trim build, and classically handsome features. But it was his eyes that caught my attention. They appeared soulful—and somehow sad.

Was he a friend of Aunt Lily's? If so, why had she never mentioned him?

A tap on my Airstream door startled me.

"Mallie? It's me," Aunt Lily called out as she swung open the door.

My gaze shifted from the picture to my real-life aunt. It took a few moments to adjust from the young image of her to the older, somewhat timeworn version. Red hair threaded with gray, freckles mixed with lines, slight sun damage covering her body. Still, in spite of her age, a radiant vitality emanated from her being. Aunt Lily would never "go gentle into that good night," as Dylan Thomas had pronounced. She'd fight every step of the way.

"I wanted to see if you'd found out anything—" She broke off as she saw the picture. A wistful expression crossed her face. Then she turned to Sam, who stood behind her. "Would you help Cole with the grilling? I need to talk to Mallie alone, please."

"Sure." I caught a brief glimpse of his squeezing her hand. He knew. Whatever this photograph was about, Sam knew.

Aunt Lily closed the door. Slowly, she moved toward me, not saying anything.

She picked up the picture, and a soft smile spread over her face. I'd never seen her looking like that. A golden glow lit her features—a glow of . . . love. "I haven't seen this in a long time." She took it over to the sofa and slowly seated herself. "I assume Maria gave it to you."

"Sort of." *Add theft to my misdemeanors.* I sat next to her. "I recognized you right away, of course. And the little girl is Mama Maria, right?"

"Yes."

"Then who's the man?"

She ran her fingers over the frame. "Maria's father—and my . . . boyfriend."

A wave of shock slapped me. "What?" For once, my motor-mouth stalled.

"I guess I need to explain." She sat back, clutching the picture. "Your Great-Uncle Rich—my husband—died during the last year of the war, somewhere in Germany. I was heart-broken. He'd been my childhood sweetheart, my friend, my companion for over ten years. Then he was dead at twenty-six. And I was left alone with a failing citrus grove and no money. That's when I met Alberto Espinosa. He managed several of the mango groves on the island. He was the one who persuaded me to convert my grove from citrus to mangos. It didn't take long for me to be in the black again—or to fall in love with Alberto."

"But I always thought you were like . . . uh . . . the grieving widow all these years."

"I was. I thought my life was over when Rich died." She sighed. "But Alberto made me want live again. He was so different from Rich. Passionate, fiery, magnetic. We argued constantly, and I couldn't resist him—or my own desires."

I swallowed hard. Aunt Lily? Desires? *Yikes.*

She patted my hand. "I know it's difficult to hear that from an old person, but I wasn't always this age. I loved two men with all my heart. Rich was my childhood sweetie, and Alberto was my mature love. I don't regret any of it."

Whew. This was heavy stuff after the crazy day I'd had. "Why did you keep it a secret all these years?"

"That's my one regret." Her face crumpled and suddenly looked old. "I know it sounds stupid in this day and age, but back then racism was alive and thriving on Coral Island. Alberto was a Latino farmer, and I was a respectable Anglo widow. Marrying him would've exposed us to dangerous repercussions. Sure, it was okay to have him manage my grove, but marry him? No. People would've never accepted it. It was easier to love him in secret."

I cast my eyes down at her wrinkled, age-spotted hand on top of mine. I turned my palm around and clasped hers. "I'm so sorry."

"Me too. I took the easy way out. I didn't follow my heart. 'Passion should believe itself irresistible.' "

"Shakespeare?"

"E.M. Forster." She laughed. "And you call yourself a comparative-literature major."

"It's been a long day."

"Poor Alberto. He never reproached me once, but it must've been so hard for him to lie and hide his feelings from others—even his own daughter."

"Mama Maria isn't your daughter?"

"I wish, but no. Maria was his daughter from his first marriage. Her mother died when Maria was born. But I loved her as if she'd been my child. I helped her start the restaurant, paid for her wedding, put Gina through decorating school. I wish I could've done more."

"You did a lot." I glanced down at the picture again. It now seemed all the more poignant because of knowing the secret that bound the three of them together. "Did Maria know?"

"I'm not sure. We never talked about it. She must've, though."

I took in a deep breath. "What happened to Alberto?"

She began to weep. "He died in the early sixties from cancer. It was one of those fast-acting, inoperable kinds. At least he didn't suffer. I don't think I could've taken seeing him in pain." She tilted her head back, fighting for control. After a minute or two, she'd mastered her emotions. "He's buried in the grove, near the first mango tree we planted together. And I've left instructions in my will that I want to be buried next to him. Please make sure that happens."

"I promise I will." I felt the sting of tears in my own eyes.

"Now you see why I was so upset about Gina's death. She was like my own grandchild. That's why we have to find who killed her."

I shook my head, trying to clear my mind of Aunt Lily's shocking revelations. *Focus. Focus.* "I guess it's okay to tell you this: you were right. Nick Billie told me this morning that a poisonous substance was found in Gina's bloodstream. He thinks someone placed it in the syringe she used to give herself insulin injections."

"I knew it!" Aunt Lily exclaimed.

"Look, I've been digging around, and while there are people who didn't *like* Gina, no one seems to have had a strong enough reason to kill her. Brandi wanted to be the Mango Queen, Brett's parents didn't like his engagement, and Isabel Morales owed her money. But none of it adds up to a real motive for murder."

"The motive may not lie in the present, but in the past."

"Do tell," I queried. She knew something else. "This isn't the time to hold back on me, Auntie."

She pursed her lips. "Right before he got cancer, Alberto told me he was going to make a lot of money—enough for us to leave the island if we wanted to. He never told me the particulars; then he got sick, and it didn't seem to matter anymore. All I know is, right about that time, Bryan Palmer's father came into a lot of cash—while Alberto managed his mango grove."

My mind raced ahead, trying to figure out the implications of what she was suggesting. "So you're saying Gina's death may be connected with something her grandfather knew?"

"Exactly."

"I hate to ask this, but . . . do you think Alberto was involved in illegal activities with the Palmers? Gunrunning, or whatever they did back then?"

"No." Her voice was firm. "Alberto would've never done anything like that."

"What, then?"

"I don't know." She shook her head negatively. "But it's nagged at me all these years—the feeling that Alberto was somehow cheated out of his rightful dues. Something that Bryan Palmer might kill to hide—"

The door to the Airstream swung open with a sudden clatter. We both jumped.

"Dinner is ready," Cole announced. His smile dimmed when he saw us. "Sorry, didn't mean to startle you."

"It's okay. We'll be right out," I said.

He closed the door quietly.

I turned to my aunt. "Are you okay?"

"Surprisingly . . . yes. It feels as if a weight has been lifted off my shoulders to be able, finally, to share the secret with you." She stood up and smoothed down her cotton top. "I'm just sorry it took such a tragic event to give me the courage to confess."

"Don't worry, I'll find out what happened to Gina. If Bryan Palmer is responsible, then he'll pay for it."

"Be careful, though. If he was willing to kill once to hide the truth, he could do it again."

Instantly, the image of the cut-up photo rose in my mind. "I . . . I may need to share this with Nick Billie."

"I know. It's okay."

"He'll be totally discreet, I'm sure."

"Oh, yes. I don't think wild horses could drag a secret out of Nick." She managed a choking laugh. "In fact, he reminds me of Alberto—passionate on the inside but strong and re-strained on the outside. He's the kind of man who'll be a rock in a storm." She winked at me.

"I like to stick to sunny weather." I reached for the door-knob, but Aunt Lily stopped me.

"Mallie, don't make the same mistake I did. Cole is nice, but is he really what you want? Love isn't comfortable. It knocks you sideways, and you're never the same again. And that's how it should be."

"You sound like Sam." Alarm bells went off inside me. "I . . . just don't know."

"Yes, you do." She touched my arm. "Don't take the easy road. You'll regret it."

I swung open the door and stepped out of the Airstream. The warm, late-afternoon sunlight greeted me. Then Cole approached, his eyes rueful as he held up a grilling utensil. "I hope I didn't burn your grouper. The fire was still a little in-tense."

"I'm sure it's fine."

But would I ever be the same after Aunt Lily's revelation? It had rocked my world.

The next two hours passed in a blur. Sam and Aunt Lily kept up a steady stream of conversation. I don't know how she did it. I was a wreck. Cole must've sensed something, because he didn't say much, either—just went about the business of serving everyone.

How could I concentrate on eating? My beloved great-aunt had had a lover, a secret that she'd hidden from me. It had been a long-term relationship, and no one in my family even knew about it. Unbelievable.

Was there anything else about her I didn't know? I kept glancing at her in dazed puzzlement.

Eventually, the dinner ended; then Aunt Lily and Sam left—she giving me a hug before they drove off. But I was still in shock.

"Are you okay?" Cole asked as we watched Sam's serviceable Volvo disappear into the twilight. Clouds had drifted in off the Gulf, and a cool breeze finally wafted in. It should've felt refreshing, but instead, it scattered my senses even further. Cole moved closer. "What's going on?"

"Just a lot of . . . stuff. I mean, I need some time to decompress. This murder case has stirred up feelings inside me, and I'm not sure how to deal with them." Not to mention I'd learned about family secrets that had shaken me right down to my Birkenstocks.

"It's cool, babe. I'll be hanging out in the van if you need to come over and talk."

"Thanks." I turned up my face and brushed my mouth against his.

He tucked my curls behind my ears. "I'm not going anywhere." *For now.* The words were unspoken, but I could hear them in my mind. As he moved toward his van, I had a mad moment of wanting to follow him, hop in, pack up, and get the hell out of there. We could take up where we'd left off in Orlando and head out for some lighthearted romance and fun.

So what if it was the "easy road"? Why did life and love have to be hard?

I took a couple of steps in Cole's direction—then halted. I couldn't just take off and leave Aunt Lily right now. She needed me to find out what had happened to Gina. Like it or not, I had taken on responsibilities on Coral Island and couldn't just toss them to the winds.

Too bad.

Sighing, I let myself into the Airstream, grabbed Kong, and made for my bed. En route, I retrieved the mango articles written by my mentally unbalanced predecessor at the *Observer.* Nothing like a couple of fruit stories to distract me and maybe even send me off to the land of nod. One could only hope.

"Whaddya think, Kong? Where should we start?"

He tapped a paw on "Mango Fever: The History of Mangos on Coral Island." *Yawn.* I sorted through the rest of the articles, which contained more of the same. No wonder the poor reporter went berserk in the Dairy Queen drive-through. She was probably half-crazy from all the excitement of writing twelve stories about a piece of fruit.

I settled into bed, Kong under one arm, and began reading. After twenty minutes, my eyelids began to droop. I'd made it through the early homesteading years when the mango groves began, right through a couple of hurricanes, the Depression, World War II . . . blah, blah, blah.

I was about to doze off when a name stood out: *Harold Palmer.*

Whoa.

Sitting up, I refocused my eyes.

The story zeroed in on the groves run by Bryan's father during the 1950s. Apparently, he'd become quite wealthy by creating new varieties of mangos: primarily Palmer's Pride, a mango that gained worldwide appeal. Palmer expanded his operation on Coral Island to include almost a thousand acres, employing over a hundred people. A picture was also included in the story, with the caption, "Harold Palmer, with his grove manager, Alberto Espinosa, and Judge Nathan Finch." They appeared relaxed and happy.

My breath caught in my throat. Aunt Lily had said that Alberto had been about to make a lot of money around the time this picture was taken. No doubt connected with Palmer. But was Finch involved?

I studied each of the men, straining to make out details in the grainy picture. They all wore short-sleeved shirts, baggy white pants, and suspenders. Alberto's dark hair and strong features stood out, as did Harold Palmer's tall, lean form. Finch, unfortunately, didn't fare so well; he had the same pinched, ferretlike face he'd passed on to his son, Homer. Bad genes have a way of staying put through the generations. Like my brother, who'd inherited the Dumbo-like ears of my father's side. Very unfortunate.

What was the secret these three men shared? Did Gina find out and end up paying with her life?

I hugged Kong even tighter. He licked my face a few times, then dropped off to sleep. Nuzzling him, I lay back, trying to calm my racing thoughts. A quick "mugatoni" meditation helped. Then, as I closed my eyes, a blast of "Nights in White Satin" emanated from the ramshackle RV next door.

Oh, no.

I rose the next morning, bleary-eyed and cranky. It had taken three calls to Pop Pop Welch to propel the aging handyman over to the hippies-from-hell next door. When he finally did show, he banged on the side of the RV with his trusty cane and threatened them with eviction.

They'd finally turned off the music. Pop Pop retreated to his golf cart, taking a couple of whiffs from his oxygen tank before he could make it back to his cottage.

After that little altercation, I managed maybe four hours of restless sleep.

I was in no mood for Bernice the next day when I rolled into the *Observer.* As I entered the office, I scanned the premises for any sign of fish bait, a tree stump, or a greasy engine. Whatever was there, I vowed it was going out the front door.

"Mallie? Can I get you a cup of coffee?" Sandy asked in a tentative voice. "You look a bit . . . out of sorts."

"Black. No sugar. No cream. And keep it coming," I growled, stalking toward my desk.

"What's going on?"

I sat down and buried my head in my hands. "Just some moronic RV-ers next to me who don't seem to realize that the Twin Palms isn't Woodstock. They cranked up the geezer rock big-time last night."

"Bummer."

"You're telling me," I mumbled.

"Here, this should help." She handed me a large, chipped mug filled to the brim with high-test, high-caffeine, hot-as-hell coffee. I raised my head and took a long, long drink. "Thanks. I needed that."

"Take this too. You need it more than I do." She set a lovely, carb-filled Krispy Kreme delight in front of me.

I gasped. "Are you sure?"

"Yep." Her sweet face beamed. "I don't need it, because I've outsmarted Butthead Bernice." She pointed at the empty cubicle.

"I'm all ears." I waited eagerly as I gulped down more coffee and bit into the doughnut.

"I thought I'd give Madame Geri's curse a little boost." She pulled up a chair, brimming with self-satisfaction. "I called Jimmy's fishing buddy, Tiko, to take Bernice out to the Seafood Shanty last night on the pretext that he might want to buy advertising for his tilapia farm. Tiko can drink a biker under the table. Anyway, they started with beer and ended up doing shots of tequila. So, after yesterday's hangover and last night's binge, Bernice is . . . out of commission." A sly smile spread across her face. "She can't even get out of bed this morning. In the meantime, I called the Finch and Harris law firm, and they want to buy advertising. Great, huh?" She held up a stand-up cardboard poster advertising the firm: LEGAL WOES? CONTACT FINCH AND

HARRIS. Tasteful. Discreet. Better yet, it didn't smell up the entire office.

"Sandy, you're a genius!" I sang out. "And send Tiko my compliments."

"Done."

As the caffeine jolted my brain out of its semistupor, something clicked. "Did you say 'Finch and Harris'?"

She nodded.

"Funny you should mention Homer Finch. In those mango articles that you gave me, there was a picture of Finch's father—"

"Old Judge Finch. He lived on Coral Island most of his life. His son, Homer, followed in his footsteps and went to law school at the University of Florida."

"I met Homer at Island Décor a few days ago. He seemed . . . surly."

"He's got the personality of a limp fish, but his advertisement did get that crummy engine out of here." Sandy positioned the poster so it faced the front door. "And he's respected enough to be one of the Mango Queen contest judges."

I blinked. "He was a judge?"

"Yup. Rumor has it that he was the deciding vote for Gina."

Homer Finch had made Gina the Mango Queen. Could it be mere coincidence?

Or something more?

Just then, the phone rang, and I picked up.

"Mallie, this is Nick Billie. I'm bringing in Rivas Fernandez for questioning in Gina's death."

I gasped. Not Rivas.

He couldn't be Gina's killer, could he?

Chapter Fourteen

Have you charged him?" I asked, my hand tightening around the receiver.

"Not formally. But his fingerprints were found on Gina's insulin testing kit and—"

"But he's her brother. It's likely that he touched the kit because they lived in the same house." I met Sandy's alarmed look. She mouthed Rivas' name, and I nodded.

"His prints were also found in Island Décor's stockroom when I investigated the possible break-in, and Isabel said he hadn't been around there for months," Nick continued.

"Oh." That was harder to explain away. "May I come by to—"

"No." His voice was firm, final.

"Then why did you call me?"

"I wanted to give you a heads-up, the promise of an exclusive story when I make an arrest, and get your agreement to pull back on any further investigations on Gina's death till I call you."

"But—"

"Mallie, I'm not asking this as the island cop, but as a . . . friend. Trust me just this once."

I raised my eyes to the ceiling in frustration. How could I turn down such an appeal? "Well . . . I've got to clear it with Bernice, and she's out today."

"Does that mean you'll sit tight?"

"Define 'tight.' "

His voice took on a distinct edge. "Stay out of trouble." He said each word slowly, carefully.

"I promise I won't do anything without calling you first." I hung up before he could respond.

"He doesn't actually think Rivas killed Gina?" Sandy asked.

"Dunno. Nick said he was only questioning him. There were incriminating fingerprints at Island Décor. . . ."

"Did you tell Nick about the phone calls and the sliced-up photo?"

I looked down at my hands, suddenly preoccupied with a dry cuticle.

"I figured you didn't. That's why I had to take matters into my own hands."

"Uh-oh." My head jerked upward. "What did you do?"

She shrugged and pursed her mouth. "I called for an expert to help protect you."

"A bodyguard?"

"Nope . . ." Just at that moment, the door was flung open, and Madame Geri strolled in, wearing a fifties-style rocka-billy dress with platform sandals—and Marley at her side, of course.

"Oh, no." I held up my hands as if to ward off an evil spirit.

"She has to cleanse your aura, or you'll be in grave danger," Sandy protested.

Madame Geri moved toward me, a black velvet bag in hand. "Everything on this island is out of balance right now—you, the mangos, the newspaper. Things are dying, withering on the vine, and we must work together to bring order back." Her words rang out forcefully. I suppose I would've taken her more seriously if she hadn't been wearing earrings in the shape of pink owls.

"Just let her do her thing—*please.*" Sandy helped her unfold a dark cloth and place it across my desk. With a flourish, Madame Geri set her bag on top and pulled out her exorcism gear.

My eyes widened as she produced a gem-studded wand, a jar of glittery dust, a tiny silver bell, and a bag of Cheetos. She opened the latter and helped herself to a few pieces, then offered some to me and Sandy. I took her up on the offer. What the heck. A few Cheetos might make the whole process easier to stomach—literally. Sandy declined.

"Is this going to take long?" I asked, eyeing the wand. That thing looked almost lethal. A couple of whaps on the head could probably knock someone out.

"As long as it needs to." Madame Geri threw some of the shimmery dust on me.

I coughed.

Then she started chanting in a low voice.

"Thank goodness Bernice couldn't make it into work today to see this. I'd never live it down." Blinking the dust away, I helped myself to another handful of Cheetos.

"Bernice's life will be very unpleasant till I take off the curse." Madame Geri reached for the wand. "No one can resist its power."

Sandy bowed her head in respect. I rolled my eyes and submitted to another sprinkling of dust. This time, I knew what was coming and closed my eyes and held my breath.

Then she picked up the wand and waved it in a series of circular motions.

Right at that point, the phone rang. No one moved. It kept on ringing.

"May I take that?" I finally piped up.

Madame Geri nodded, without a pause in her chanting.

I picked up the receiver, careful not to entangle the cord in Madame Geri's wand. "Hello?"

"Mallie? This is Isabel Morales."

I took in a quick breath. "Did you find something?"

"Did I ever! I played around on Gina's laptop till I figured out her password: *honeybuns*. That's what she called Brett: her honeybuns."

Jeez.

"You were right; she kept a second set of accounts on it. The missing bill she invoiced the morning she died was from Homer Finch for a full day of 'legal services.' " She paused. "Gina paid him only a hundred and fifty dollars."

"That's all? Attorneys make more than that per hour." My brow knit in puzzlement. "Then Homer's bill had to be for something else . . . something he wanted to hide. Could it be connected with your decorating business? Had Gina asked Homer to do some legal work for Island Décor?"

"No. I would've known about that. Gina and I made all our business decisions together."

"Then it had to be personal," I mused. Madame Geri upped the volume on her chant and began to ring the bell right next to the receiver. Groaning inwardly, I shifted the phone to the opposite ear.

"What? I didn't hear you," Isabel exclaimed.

"Sorry. Madame Geri is doing some kind of aura cleansing—"

"Wow. You lucky girl. I've tried to get her to do me forever. She's booked almost a year ahead."

"Yeah, fortune is smiling down on me."

Madame Geri covered me with another wave of glitter dust. The wand circled faster and faster. Marley flapped his wings. I was getting dizzy and could barely breathe.

"Okay, that's enough—I can't think or hear." I jumped to my feet, placing a hand over the receiver's mouthpiece.

Madame Geri halted ringing the bell. "But I'm not finished."

"I don't care. I'd prefer having a dirty aura to this New Age nuttiness." I held up the phone as if it were a talisman warding her off. "Now, back away."

Madame Geri drew up to her full five-foot-two height and glared at me, and Marley seemed to mirror her affronted expression. Then, she took a step backward.

"Mallie? Mallie?" Isabel's voice came through the phone with a muffled sound.

"I'm here." I kept a wary eye on our resident psychic. "Um . . . make a copy of the bill, and take it over to Detective Billie. He'll want to see it right away."

She agreed and hung up. I needed to talk to Mama Maria again. She might know why Gina had hired Homer.

Madame Geri set the wand and bell on the velvet square. The glitter-dust jar was empty. "The only reason I stopped is because the spirit world directed me to. They told me that your aura is your destiny, and it needs to remain unchanged."

"What does that mean?"

"You're on the path you need to be on."

Ironically, I felt let down. "After all that rigmarole, I'm not even partially cleansed?"

She folded up the psychic paraphernalia inside the velvet cloth. "I placed a protection spell on you. That may help."

"Gee, thanks."

"What about the mango balance?" Sandy rushed to help her tidy up the rest of her aura-cleansing gear.

Madame Geri's mouth turned down. "The island fruit will not flourish till the murderer is brought to justice." She turned to me. "I'm ready."

"For what?"

"To go with you to see Mama Maria." She tucked her bag under her arm, keeping Marley close. "Let's roll."

I gritted my teeth. How in the world did she do that? I absolutely and unequivocally refused to believe that she was the real deal. I'd worked a psychic hotline as one of my many undistinguished jobs, and I knew for certain that those Miss Mystic Wannabees couldn't foretell a hurricane if they were standing in gale-force winds. "Just keep that bird under control. I don't want him messing up my truck."

"That *would* be a crime." Madame Geri stroked his turquoise feathers.

"Hey, watch it. My poor old truck, Rusty, is doing the best he can. So he's had some deterioration. I like to see what you'd look like after pulling a four-thousand-pound Airstream."

"Uh-huh." Madame Geri pivoted and headed for the door. I followed her out to Rusty. We both climbed in and immediately rolled down the windows, the heat from the seats enveloping us in a suffocating embrace. Even Marley seemed to droop a bit.

I cranked the engine. After a few attempts, it roared into life and provided a meager wisp of air-conditioning. We left the windows partially lowered.

"By the way, anyone could've guessed that I was heading to Mama Maria's."

Madame Geri said nothing.

"It makes sense. I needed more information about Gina."

Her silence continued.

"A child could've predicted that."

She smiled.

Drat her anyway.

By the time we pulled up to Mama Maria's restaurant, it was close to lunchtime. The lovely aroma of fried food wafted out and assailed my senses, and for a moment, I was lost in a fantasy of burritos, tacos, and enchiladas. Yum.

Then I remembered why we were there.

I parked Rusty and took a few seconds to gather my thoughts. "I don't want to upset Mama Maria, but I need to know why Gina hired Homer Finch to do legal work for her."

"You can count on Marley and me to help. I'll know just what to say."

Oh, goody.

We entered the restaurant and caused an immediate stir among several lunchtime diners. I knew better than to think I had much to do with the reaction. It was Madame Geri. People practically bowed in awed respect everywhere she went on the island. I found it irritating as all get-out, but what the heck? People preferred phony psychics to nosy reporters any day.

"Is Mama Maria around?" I asked one of the teenage waitresses. She had blond hair and a sweet face.

"Round back in her house, I think," the young girl said. "She got really upset this morning when the policeman came for Rivas."

"Oh, no." I motioned Madame Geri to follow me through to the back door.

The blond placed a hand on my companion's arm. "Madame Geri, my boyfriend, Buzzy, says he doesn't want to get married. Do you think I should stick around and wait till he's ready?"

Madame Geri paused, presumably for an instant message from the spirit world. "You might need to move on. . . . Sorry, my dear."

The girl's lower lip quivered, and tears filmed her eyes. "I knew that. But I just didn't want to believe it."

"Real love is right under your nose. Your neighbor T.J. is available—and interested."

Dawning realization touched the blond's face, causing a wide smile to appear. "Oh, my, you're so right. He's been there all the time. Thank you so much."

I restrained myself from commenting.

Before Madame Geri could rearrange anyone else's life, we exited the restaurant and found Mama Maria standing just inside the screen door of her house. "I knew you'd come. You heard about Rivas."

"Are you doing okay?" I moved toward her.

She opened the door and gestured for us to enter. "He wasn't arrested. Nick made that *muy claro*—very clear. Still, I'm worried. Rivas has a temper. He could say something that would make the police suspicious. But he would never have hurt Gina—he loved her. The police took Rivas in because they think someone k . . . k . . ." Her face crumpled, and the words wouldn't come.

"No need to say it. We know," I reassured her.

"Madame Geri. It's an honor," Mama Maria said, giving a little incline of her head as we stepped into the house.

Oh, not her too.

Madame Geri then did something that surprised me: she gave Mama Maria a hug—and I could swear that stupid bird even curled his wings around the grieving mother. Maybe I was beginning to semi-hallucinate.

"Mama Maria, I need to talk with you," I broke in, swallowing hard. The last thing I wanted to do was press her for information, but it had to be done. "This must be incredibly hard, with your daughter having died a few days ago and now Rivas taken into the police station. But I need to ask you a few questions. They may seem a little odd, and you don't have to answer if you don't want to, but it would help. My job is to find out what happened, and I have a lead of sorts—"

Marley squawked.

"Keep him quiet," I whispered.

"He will—if you can get to the point." Madame Geri led Mama Maria to a small sofa.

"I can't help it. All the tension from today has shifted my motormouth into overdrive."

Seating myself next to Mama Maria, I took her hand and clasped it tightly. "Let me try to be brief. Whoever did this awful thing to Gina is still out there, and I think I know who did it."

Her hand tightened around my palm.

"Let me ask you a question: Did you ever hear Gina talking to Homer Finch on the phone?"

Surprise touched her face. "Homer?" Her head tilted down as she tried to remember. Minutes passed in silence. "I . . . I don't think so."

"Did she mention his name at all?" I pressed.

"Uh . . . no. Wait, yes, she did." Mama Maria's head came up. "When she was reading about the history of Coral Island's mango groves, she asked me about Papa's connection with Mr. Harold Palmer and Judge Nathan Finch. They worked together years ago in the Palmer groves."

"Did anything . . . unusual happen during that time when your father worked in the Palmer groves?"

She shrugged. "I was just a girl then. And Papa got sick soon after."

"Were the men working on any kind of special project together?" I continued to push for answers. There *had* to be a connection. "Something that could've made Palmer a lot of money? If so, your father might've been too sick to care, and Judge

Finch was probably only too happy to cut him out of the profits. Gina may have found out and then hired Homer as a smoke-screen for confronting him."

"That doesn't make sense," Madame Geri pointed out.

So my theory wasn't foolproof. "All I know is, Gina paid Homer a small amount of money the morning she died, and it wasn't the usual legal fee."

Mama Maria rubbed her eyes in weariness. "This is all so confusing. How can anything so far in the past relate to Gina's death?"

"My editor, Anita, always says 'follow the money,' and it's been my experience so far that she's right. People will do almost anything when it comes to making big bucks."

"The spirit world has told me almost the same thing," Madame Geri added—quite unnecessarily.

"Okay, Mama Maria, let's brainstorm," I said. "Do you remember how the Palmers made all their money?"

"*Sí.* They created new types of mangos that grew better and tasted sweeter than any others. One was the best mango I'd ever eaten: Palmer's Pride. It tastes like no other mango—like coconut and cinnamon."

Something clicked in the back of my mind. The mango slices that Gina gave me on the trail had those exact flavors Mama Maria just described. "I think I've had that mango."

"Not possible." Mama Maria waved a finger in dissent. "The Palmers don't sell it locally. It's prized all over the world, so they send it only to special places in Europe and Asia."

"What does it look like?"

"Different from most mangos—very pale, almost milky-colored instead of the usual deep peachy-yellow."

"Oh, yes!" I almost clapped. "Gina gave me some of that mango on the trail, the morning she died. Did she have it when she left the house?"

"No. I would've known."

"Where could she get some?"

"Only at the Palmer groves." Mama Maria's startled eyes locked onto mine. "She must've gone there before she had breakfast at the restaurant."

I rose and began to pace the room, trying to piece together a theory. "So, first thing in the morning, Gina went to the Palmer groves and met Homer Finch. She gave him cash for some kind of legal services, picked up a few mango slices . . . and somehow a toxic pesticide wound up in her syringe." My heart began to beat faster. "Of course, they'd have pesticides at a mango grove. It makes sense. Somehow, Homer got hold of Gina's purse and tampered with her insulin kit."

"Homer Finch? It still feels wrong to me," Madame Geri chimed in.

I gave her a dismissive wave. "The spirit world doesn't know everything."

Madame Geri snorted.

"I'm going over to the Palmers' groves to see if I can find any evidence." I grabbed my canvas bag.

"Shouldn't you call Nick Billie first?" Mama Maria inquired, wringing her hands.

"Not yet. All I've got is a theory. Let me see what I can dig up, and then I'll call him. Nobody knows that we've figured out Homer Finch's connection to Gina's death, so we've got a little time. Hopefully, Homer left some kind of evidence that we can use to clear Rivas." I smiled down at Mama Maria. "Don't worry. I can take care of myself."

"I'm coming with you," Madame Geri announced.

"No, stay here with Mama Maria. She needs you more than I do. I'll drive to the Palmers' groves, look around, and be right back, okay?"

Madame Geri frowned. "The spirit world urges caution."

"Not to worry." I raised my chin in a show of pride. "I'm a trained professional journalist—and I have martial-arts training. I know exactly where I'm going and what I'm doing." Swinging my bag onto my shoulder, I strode toward the door. Then, I paused and turned. "Uh . . . where *are* the Palmers' groves?"

Madame Geri sighed.

About thirty minutes later, with a couple of wrong turns (Mama Maria's directions were a bit imprecise), I found myself lurching down a two-lane shell road that I'd never driven before.

The mango groves were located south of the island center in a heavily agricultural area. Palm-tree farms mixed with exotic nurseries, herb fields, and mango groves. Needless to say, the roads had potholes that seemed more like black holes. Rusty lurched and teetered. As my body pitched back and forth, I prayed we made it there intact.

Since I'd never even purchased a potted plant, I had no reason to frequent this part of Coral Island. And, after today, I vowed never to return if all my organs survived the punishing ride.

Eventually, I spotted a sign decorated with multicolored mangos that read PALMER'S GROVE. Unlike the places I'd just passed, this acreage appeared very well kept. A row of neatly trimmed areca palms stretched across the front of the property, interspersed with decorative bougainvillea bushes. Beyond, vast rows of mango trees stretched in either direction as far as I could see.

I parked Rusty in front of a small frame building and looked around. The place seemed deserted for lunchtime.

Perfect.

I could look around without any encumbrances.

Sliding out of my truck, I gave my cell phone a quick check to see that I had plenty of battery power. That way, if anything happened, I had Nick Billie on speed dial.

I moved toward the building, inhaling the balmy aroma of mangos. Stronger than a scented flower, deeper than a perfume. The fruits were everywhere. Scattered under the trees, heaped in wooden crates, stacked in boxes. Mangotown.

Remembering the luscious taste of the mango slices still in my fridge, my mouth began to water. I touched one; it was soft and ripe, almost mushy, and ready to eat. *Maybe later.*

Tapping on the door, I took another nervous glance around. Nick Billie would pitch a fit if he knew I was trespassing on Palmer land just to find evidence. But I had to know the truth about Homer Finch's involvement in Gina's death.

When no one answered, I found the door unlocked and slipped inside. For a few moments, I gulped in the air-conditioning provided by a small window unit. Gamely, it chugged along, lowering the temperature from ninety-five degrees to a cool ninety—marginal improvement at best.

I glanced around. The building appeared little more than a large, unfinished storage shed. A long counter stood in the middle of the room with postal scales and sealing tape on top. Sample bags of mango slices, similar to the one Gina had the day she died, layered the bottom of a wooden tray. *Proof.* And I had Gina's bag in my fridge. I swiped a couple more—for evidence, of course.

Then I threaded my way through shipping boxes with the label PALMER'S PRIDE that littered the floor. Obviously, this was the spot where the Palmers dispatched their famous mango.

What about the pesticide?

Shelves lined the back of one wall, stocked with various agricultural paraphernalia, from pruning sheers to Weedwhackers. I methodically checked each shelf, one by one, for a pesticide container but found nothing. The adjacent room held mango-filled boxes, ready to be mailed out. Nothing again.

Damn.

Maybe this *was* just a shipping center. But Gina had to have stopped here the morning she died, and it was the only opportunity Homer had to put the pesticide in her syringe.

I checked my Mickey Mouse watch. Almost 1:00 P.M. People would be trailing back from lunch, so I had to get out of there.

As I pivoted to leave, I spied a small bathroom off to the left of the counter. Hesitating, I checked my watch again. Okay, I had time for a peek.

I entered the tiny room and did a quick scan. Plain white toilet (not too clean) and cabinet with sink (even dirtier). *Ick.* I opened the cabinet doors and found only a stack of paper towels. As I was about to close the doors, something caught my eye.

A plastic container.

My heart began to beat a little faster. I took one of the paper towels and edged the bottle out, so as to not tamper with any fingerprints. The label read PESTICIDE: DANGEROUS IF SWALLOWED. Evidence?

All I had to do was call Nick Billie and get him over here to secure a sample and see if it matched the pesticide found in Gina's blood.

I reached for my cell phone but couldn't get a signal. Leaving the pesticide container, I rushed back into the main shipping room, frantically pressing the buttons on my cell phone.

"What are you doing here?" a man's voice asked.

I looked up. It was Homer Finch.

Uh-oh.

Chapter Fifteen

I ... I might ask you the same question," I stammered. He didn't appear to have a weapon. That, at least, was good news.

"You found out, didn't you?" he inquired, his ferretlike face taut with strain.

"I don't know what you mean. I came here to ... uh ... pick up some mangos. See?" I held up the plastic bags. "These Palmer's Prides are delicious. I've never tasted anything like it. I mean, the mango wasn't really my favorite fruit, but once I tried this, I was hooked. The blend of flavors is like something—"

"Shut up."

"Okay." I bit my lip. Not the time for the motormouth to kick in. It seemed to irritate most people—especially those on the verge of admitting to murder. "I'll just put these away." I placed the mango samples into my canvas bag, along with the cell phone—but not before I'd surreptitiously punched Nick Billie's speed-dial number again. "How did you know I'd be here?"

"I heard Isabel call you about the messy desk. I figured something was up, so I drove to the *Observer* and followed you from there to Mama Maria's and, finally, here," he explained in a smug voice. "You know, my storage closet at Finch and Harris is right next to Island Décor's stockroom, so I can hear everything that goes on in there through the ventilation system. It's been mildly interesting over the last few years." He still hadn't made a move in my direction. "I thought I'd gotten rid of all the evidence when I stole the invoice and wiped Gina's hard drive clean. Sadly, I was mistaken."

"Why did you do it, HOMER?" I said in a loud voice, hoping Nick could hear on the other end of the cell phone.

"I'm not a thief. I came here to try to tell my side." Homer spread his arms in appeal. "I knew if anyone found that invoice, they might question my integrity—and Gina's rightful title as Mango Queen. That poor, sweet girl. She had so much life ahead of her."

"You regret what happened. I know. And the police will take that into account, I'm sure." I cleared my throat audibly. "But you didn't answer my question. WHY DID YOU KILL GINA?"

"What are you saying?" His features became more pinched. "I didn't kill her."

"YES, YOU DID."

"No, I didn't."

"THEN WHY DID YOU STEAL THE INVOICE?"

"Because I thought someone might think I rigged the Mango Queen pageant. Gina paid me a hundred and fifty dollars the day after she became the queen—that would look suspicious to anyone. But she won fair and square. Gina deserved to be Mango Queen."

I blinked back my puzzlement. "WHAT IS THE INVOICE FOR?"

"Why are you shouting? I'm standing right here."

"Oh, sorry. I . . . do that when I get nervous. I talk a lot—and loudly."

"The invoice was for her pre-nup."

"Huh?"

"She hired me to write up a prenuptial contract for her marriage to Brett Palmer," he explained. "That's why I met her the day she died. She wanted to pay me for the legal work."

"That's it?"

"'Fraid so."

I stared at him, still confused. "What about the pesticide?"

He shook his head. "You've lost me there."

"You know Gina was diabetic?"

"Yes, that's what killed her."

I drilled him with my stare. "No, she died because of a toxic pesticide someone put into her insulin syringe."

His mouth dropped open. "But . . . but . . . I thought she died from diabetes complications. Sure, I heard some rumors around the island, but I didn't believe them. I mean, who could've harmed Gina—" He broke off, an expression of horror crossing his face. "You don't think that *I* would've done something like that?"

"You met her here the morning she died. And the pesticide they found in her body was the brand used on mango trees—like the kind I found back there in a cupboard." I pointed in the direction of the bathroom.

"It wasn't me, I swear!" he cried out.

"ARE YOU SAYING YOU DIDN'T KILL GINA, HOMER?" I tilted my face toward the canvas bag, just to make certain it got through on the cell phone.

"I'm not deaf, you idiot."

"Oh, sorry." I checked the window, but no sign of Nick Billie yet. "Why don't you turn yourself in?"

"I told you, I didn't kill Gina." His voice took on a note of anguish as he slumped into a chair and dropped his head into his hands. "Oh, God. I never dreamed that she could harm Gina—"

"Who are you taking about? Do you know who did it? Are you protecting someone?"

His head shot up.

Pay dirt.

"Homer, if you know anything, you need to tell me," I urged. "Rivas Fernandez was taken in for questioning this morning. You can't let an innocent man take the rap for a crime he didn't commit." I knelt down next to him. "Was there someone else here the morning you met Gina?"

"Maybe."

"Who? WHO ELSE WAS HERE WHEN YOU MET GINA?"

Homer began to whimper.

"Jeez, I've heard enough of this crap," Trish Palmer said in a disgusted tone as she strolled into the room from the rear door. She leveled a gun at me, throwing a momentary glance of derision in Homer's direction. "You gutless weasel."

I straightened, my legs slightly unsteady. Her eyes glittered with a hard, unbalanced edge—the kind of look I used to get from half-crazed parents who'd dragged their kids around Disney World all day and were ready to take out Mickey Mouse at any cost. I was in deep trouble.

"TRISH PALMER. WHAT ARE YOU DOING HERE?" Sweat broke out across my forehead. "WHY DO YOU HAVE THAT GUN?"

"Pipe down."

Homer whimpered more loudly.

"Why did you do it, Trish?" I asked quietly. "Because of Brett?"

"Pffft. She could have Brett. He never would've made senator. He's too damn nice." She ground out the last word as if it were a vicious insult. "I killed her because she could ruin us. She'd found out that it was her grandfather who developed Palmer's Pride—"

"And was swindled out of its big profits." I checked the window again. Still no sign of Nick. Where was he? "How much money are we talking about?"

"More than you could imagine." Her carefully outlined lips curled. "I was trailer trash just like you when I married into the Palmer family. I wanted all the things Bryan could give me: the money, the mansion, the jewels. And I don't intend to give them up. When I saw a copy of the pre-nup in Homer's office, I realized Gina was a threat to my little world, and I wasn't about to let her bring it down. Bryan didn't know, of course. Not about Alberto's patent for Palmer's Pride or Gina's pre-nup stating that she would receive all the mango profits if she and Brett divorced." Her voice took on a hard edge. "I knew Brett was besotted enough to sign that thing, so I had to get rid of her before he had a chance to see it."

"You're nuts." I glared at her, still smarting from being called "trailer trash."

"It's all my fault," Homer whined. "I should've never told you about that pre-nup."

"Darn right, and you also shouldn't have told me that you had an appointment right here with Gina early that morning—and allowed me to come with you," she added with a sly smile. "After you left, she and I had a pleasant conversation about Alberto's patent—and the 'mix-up' all those years ago. She didn't buy it. So, when she was on her cell phone, I put the pesticide into her syringe. It was surprisingly easy."

"Damn you," Homer said in a weak voice.

"I think that's a given," I muttered, taking a quick inventory for possible weapons. Nothing was within arm's reach. "WHAT ARE YOU GONNA DO, TRISH? KILL US BOTH?"

"Stop shouting, you moron." She produced a sheet of stationery with Finch & Harris' letterhead. "What a shame Homer felt so desperate about being discovered as Gina's killer that he had to shoot you and then himself. Not to worry. He sets it all out in this suicide note." She waved the paper. "Oh, and I also took the other pre-nup copies out of your files."

"You'll never get away with it," I said with more bravado than I was feeling.

"Oh, yes, I will. And it's your own fault for meddling. I tried to scare you off with the phone calls and the slashed picture, but you wouldn't back off."

"It's my job. Bernice made me do it." Okay, that was lame, but I was growing desperate. I inched back from Homer, finding nothing but a crate of very ripe mangos at my fingertips.

"Too bad." She pointed the gun at Homer. "All right. You first, nitwit."

He jumped to his feet. "You think you're so smart. I already sent a copy of the pre-nup to Brett. He's probably looking at it right now."

"You didn't!" Her face contorted with rage.

"Yes, I did!"

Trish lost it. She lunged at him.

I instantly sprang into action, grabbing a couple of mangos. I flung them at her, and they splattered all over her white silk pantsuit. She was so startled at the sight of mango goop, she dropped the gun.

Now it was my turn to lunge. I grasped a few more mangos and smashed them into her chest. She went down, with me on top of her. "HOMER, PICK UP THE GUN!"

Trish cursed me and ground a stray mango into my face. I

sputtered but held my position. Her arms and legs were flailing, and she tried to claw at my face. I spit out the pulp and rammed a big Palmer's Pride into her eyes.

She yelped.

We wrestled around in the mango mush for what seemed an eternity as I kept yelling for Homer's help.

Finally, a strong hand pulled me off Trish.

"You sure took your sweet time, Homer." I brushed my mango-drenched hair out of my face to behold Nick Billie. "Oh, thank goodness. I guess you heard me on the cell phone—pretty smart, huh?"

"No, you dialed Wanda Sue by mistake. That's why I wasn't here sooner—she had to patch the call through to me." He slapped a pair of handcuffs onto Trish. "It would've been nice to give me a heads-up before you swung into action, but I think you've been punished enough." He glanced at my disheveled appearance, and amusement mingled with annoyance on his face. "I thought we agreed to use teamwork."

"You want to work with *her*?" Trish wiped mango shreds off her jacket. "Trailer-trash girl?"

"It takes one to know one," I retorted.

"That's enough, Mrs. Palmer," Nick said in a grim voice. "You're being arrested on suspicion of murder. I'd be worried about *that,* if I were you."

"She did it, all right." Homer waved the gun at Trish for emphasis.

We all ducked.

"Give me that gun," Nick ordered.

Homer immediately complied.

"Mallie, you and Homer follow me to the police station, where I'll take your statements." He led Trish Palmer to the door.

"What about Rivas?" I asked.

"He's fine. I brought him in because I was getting closer to arresting Trish, and I thought he might go ballistic if he knew that one of the Palmers had killed his sister. She and Homer were my prime suspects, because two migrant workers reported seeing both of them here the morning Gina died. Once I knew a pesticide killed her, I figured one of them did it. I was on my way here to gather evidence when Wanda Sue interrupted me with your call."

"So that whole thing about Rivas' fingerprints was phony?"

He gave me a sheepish grin.

"So much for 'teamwork.' " I placed my hands on my hips. "I guess we're never going to see eye to eye, are we?"

"Probably not." He leaned down and planted a brief, searing kiss on my mouth. "Then again, maybe we don't need to."

As he ushered Trish Palmer out of the building, I stood still, shocked.

"Call me if you need a good pre-nup." Homer Finch handed me his card.

"Shut up." I followed them out, climbed into Rusty, and drove off.

Epilogue

Would you like a piece of mango, Mallie?" Wanda Sue passed a slice across my picnic table.

"No, thanks. I don't think I can look at that particular fruit again for a long time." It had taken me three washings with Kong's favorite shampoo to get the last of the slimy mango goop out of my hair.

As for my skin, the sunburn had finally faded to a soft pink, though I did have a new smattering of freckles across my nose.

"At least the trees are healthy again," Aunt Lily pointed out. The three of us looked toward a small private grove behind the RV park. Large mangos hung on every limb, bursting with color and ripeness, luscious and enticing.

Except to me.

"Madame Geri says the island's mango balance has been restored," Wanda Sue murmured. "Thank the good Lord."

"And Mallie." Aunt Lily smiled at me. A shadow of sadness still lingered around her eyes, but now that the truth was out about Alberto's patent, peace had found its way there too. Her personal history with him remained private.

"How's Mama Maria?" I patted her hand.

"Surviving. That's about all she'll be able to do for a while, but that's something," Aunt Lily said. "I'll be there for her every step of the way."

We fell silent. It seemed too soon to be lighthearted. Gina still had to be mourned.

"Hello, ladies," Cole said as he ducked under my awning. "Are you ready for the Mango Festival?"

"I plumb forgot that today's the day," Wanda Sue declared. "We have to go—for Gina's sake. You know they decided to keep her as the posthumous queen, and even Brandi was okay with it."

"That's excellent." Cole stood behind me and brushed a light kiss on my head. It should've felt comforting, but, instead, it reminded me of the burning excitement of Nick Billie's lips. Heat rose up my neck, and I picked up an empty paper plate and briefly fanned myself.

"Don't you have to cover the festival for the *Observer*?" Aunt Lily inquired.

"I didn't get the assignment—hah! Apparently, when Bernice was recovering from her second hangover a couple of days ago, she tripped over an empty beer bottle and broke her ankle. Tragic." I shook my head in mock sorrow. "Anyway, she'll be out of commission till Anita gets back, and I'm using the break from both of them as an opportunity to take a little vacation." I stretched my arms behind my head with a self-satisfied expression.

"Madame Geri's curse strikes again," Aunt Lily sang out.

Wanda Sue crossed herself.

Just then, geezer rock burst forth once more from the ramshackle RV next door. "That's it. I've had it." I walked over and pounded on the siding. "Get out here and show yourselves, you aging hippie jerks!"

Laughter erupted, and I heard a door open. Two sets of bare feet came around the front of the tenement on wheels.

"Anita!" I exclaimed as I spied her saddlebag-brown face.

"Hi, kiddo." Her arm was linked through Mr. Benton's. He beamed as if he'd just spent a week with Cameron Diaz. *Jeez.*

"You're the ones who've been playing that loud rock day and night?"

Cole placed a hand on my shoulder.

She cackled. "Guilty as charged."

"Do you know what's been going on this last week? Murder and mayhem! And I couldn't even get any rest at night," I ranted. "What with Gina's death, Butthead Bernice in charge, Trish Palmer's arrest—"

"Aw, muzzle it," Anita cut me off. "I heard that Madame Geri put a curse on my sister, and now she's laid up. That's a shame. And it means I have to take charge again. Vacation is over, kiddo. You need to get your butt in gear and cover the Mango Festival today. I want full coverage—photos, interviews, you name it. Let's get cracking." She snapped her fingers. "I'm baacccccck."

Oh, boy.